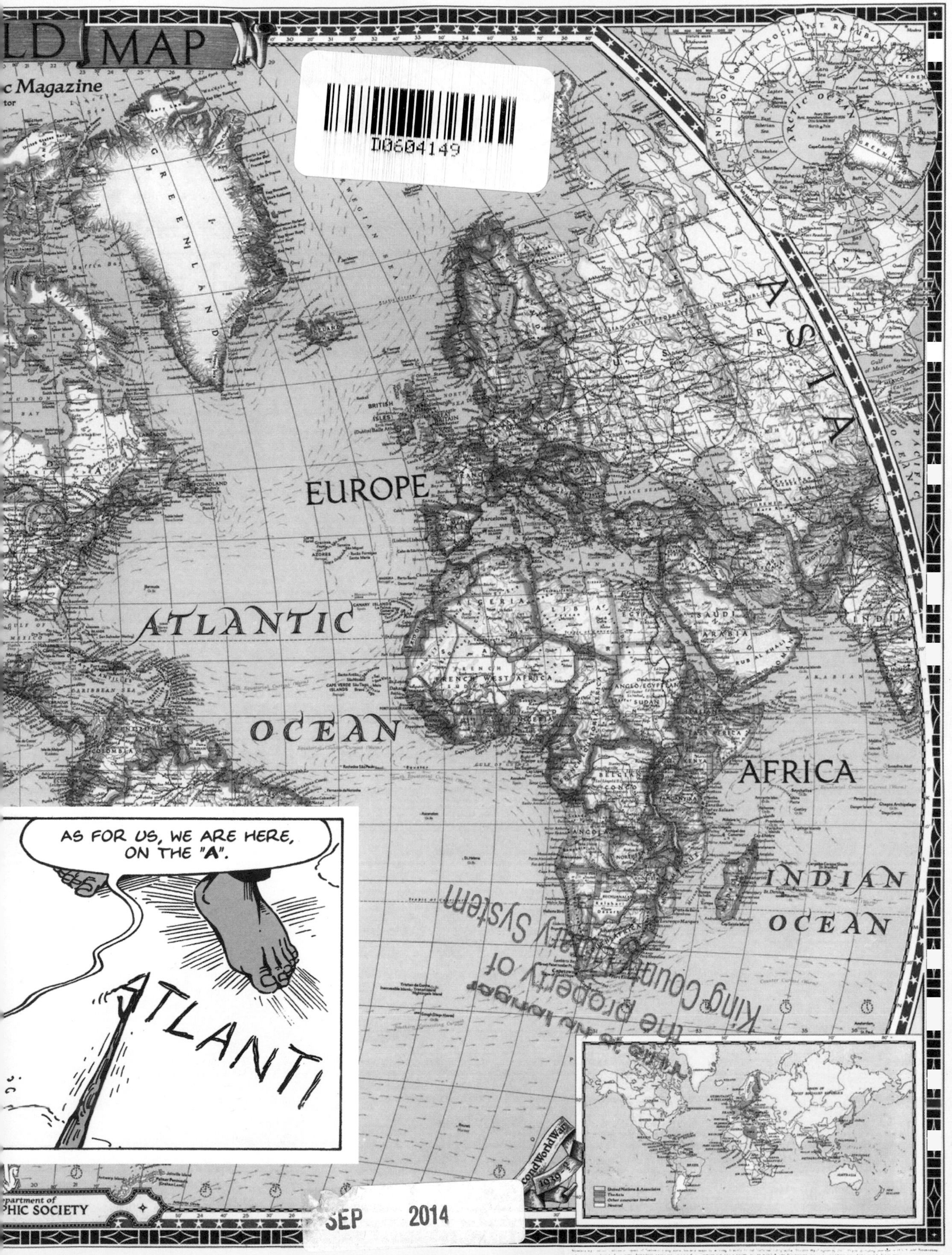
LD MAP
c Magazine
GREENLAND
EUROPE
ASIA
ATLANTIC
OCEAN
AFRICA
INDIAN
OCEAN
BRITISH ISLES
ARCTIC OCEAN
FRENCH WEST AFRICA
ALGERIA
SAUDI ARABIA
SUDAN
BELGIAN CONGO
ANGOLA
CARIBBEAN SEA
AZORES
CANARY ISLANDS
CAPE VERDE ISLANDS
NORWEGIAN SEA
BLACK SEA
PACIFIC OCEAN
INDIA
partment of
PHIC SOCIETY
Second World War
1939
AS FOR US, WE ARE HERE, ON THE "A".
ATLANTI

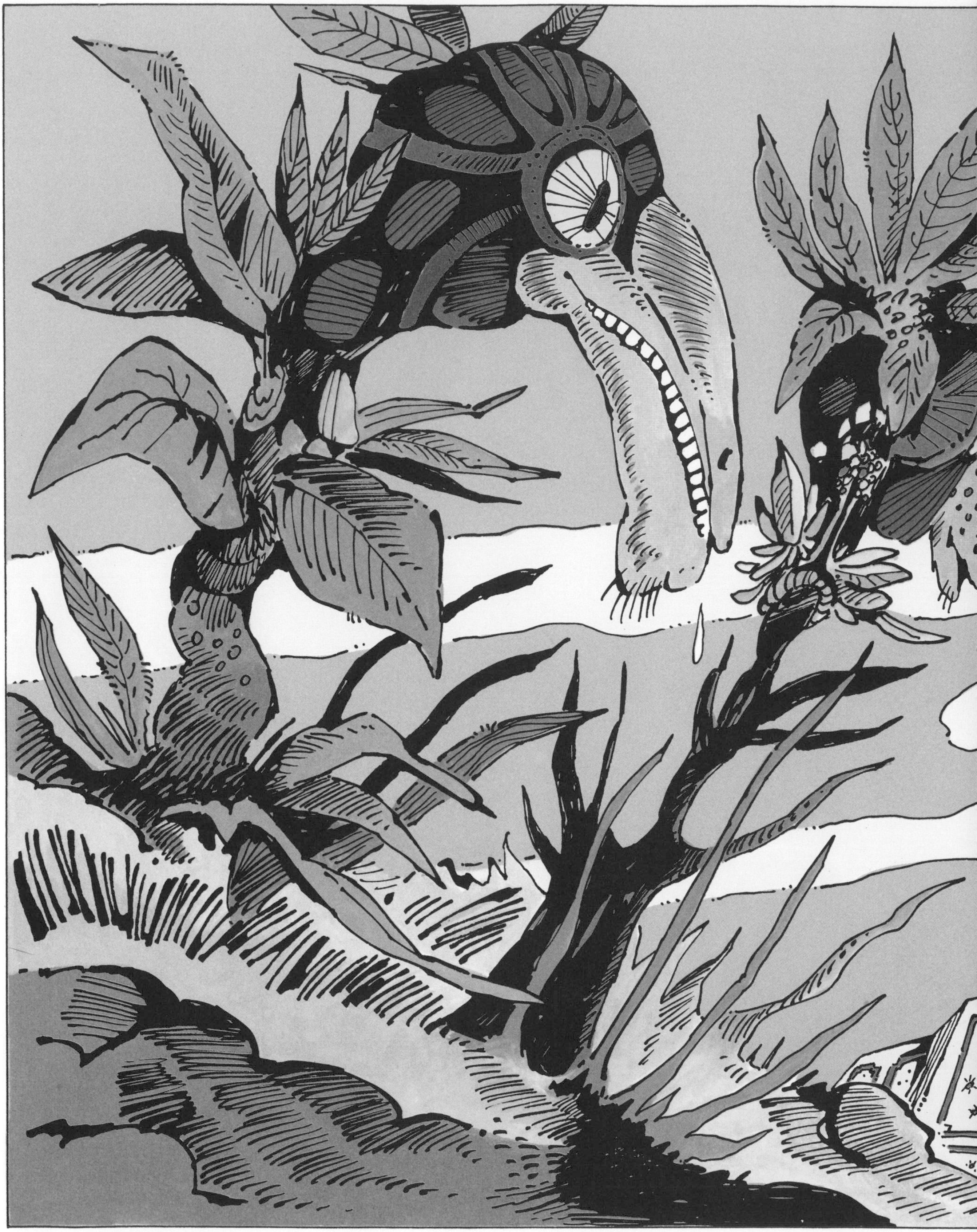

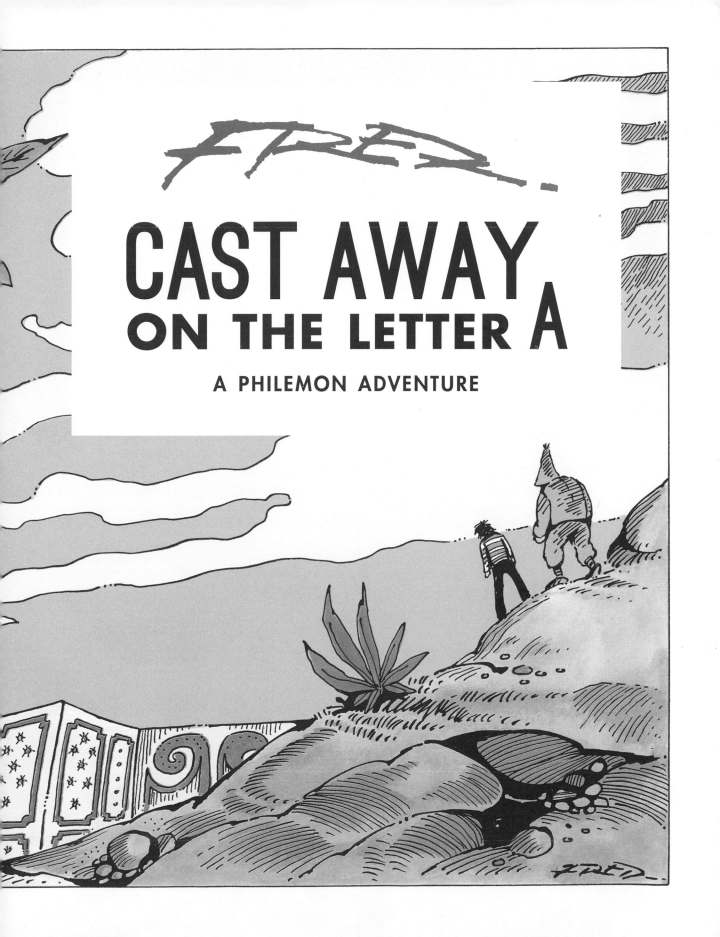

CAST AWAY
ON THE LETTER A
A PHILEMON ADVENTURE

Editorial Director: FRANÇOISE MOULY

Book Design: FRANÇOISE MOULY & JONATHAN BENNETT

Translation: RICHARD KUTNER

Hand-lettering: MYKEN BOMBERGER & FRED

FRED'S artwork was drawn in India ink, watercolor and gouache.

FOR VISUAL READERS
TOON
GRAPHICS

A TOON Graphic™ © 2014 RAW Junior, LLC, 27 Greene Street, New York, NY 10013. TOON Books® is an imprint of Candlewick Press, 99 Dover Street, Somerville, MA 02144. Original text and illustrations from *Philémon et le naufragé du A,* © 1972 DARGAUD. Translation, ancillary material, and TOON Graphic™ adaptation © 2014 RAW Junior, LLC. We gratefully acknowledge the support of the MCUFEU (Mission culturelle et universitaire française aux Etats-Unis). World map courtesy of the National Geographic Society. No part of this book may be used or reproduced in any manner whatsoever without written permission except in the case of brief quotations embodied in critical articles and reviews. TOON Graphics™, TOON Books®, LITTLE LIT® and TOON Into Reading!™ are trademarks of RAW Junior, LLC. All rights reserved. Printed in China by C&C Offset Printing Co., Ltd.

Library of Congress Cataloging-in-Publication Data:

Fred, 1931- author, illustrator.   [Philémon et le naufragé du A. English]   Cast away on the letter A: a Philemon adventure / by Fred; translated by Richard Kutner.   pages cm. – (TOON Graphics) Originally published by Dargaud in 1972 under title: Philémon et le naufragé du A.   SUMMARY: "Young dreamer Philemon lives in the countryside, until one day he falls down a well and finds himself in a parallel world of islands that form the letters of the word Atlantic Ocean. Together with the strange characters he meets there, Philemon must find his way home" – Provided by publisher.

ISBN 978-1-935179-63-4 (hardcover) 1. Graphic novels. [1. Graphic novels. 2. Adventure and adventurers–Fiction. 3. Escapes–Fiction. 4. Islands–Fiction. 5. Alphabet–Fiction.] I. Kutner, Richard, translator. II. Title. PZ7.7.F73Ph 2014   741.5'944–dc23   2013047986

14 15 16 17 18 19 C&C 10 9 8 7 6 5 4 3 2 1

CAST AWAY ON THE LETTER A

A PHILEMON ADVENTURE

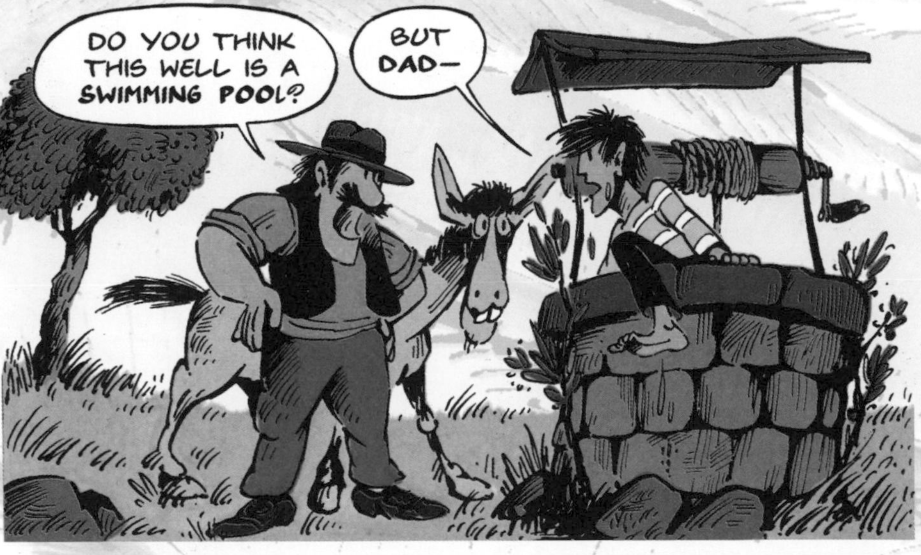
DO YOU THINK THIS WELL IS A SWIMMING POOL?
BUT DAD—

A TOON GRAPHIC BY

FRED

TOON BOOKS IS AN IMPRINT OF CANDLEWICK PRESS

MEET PHILEMON

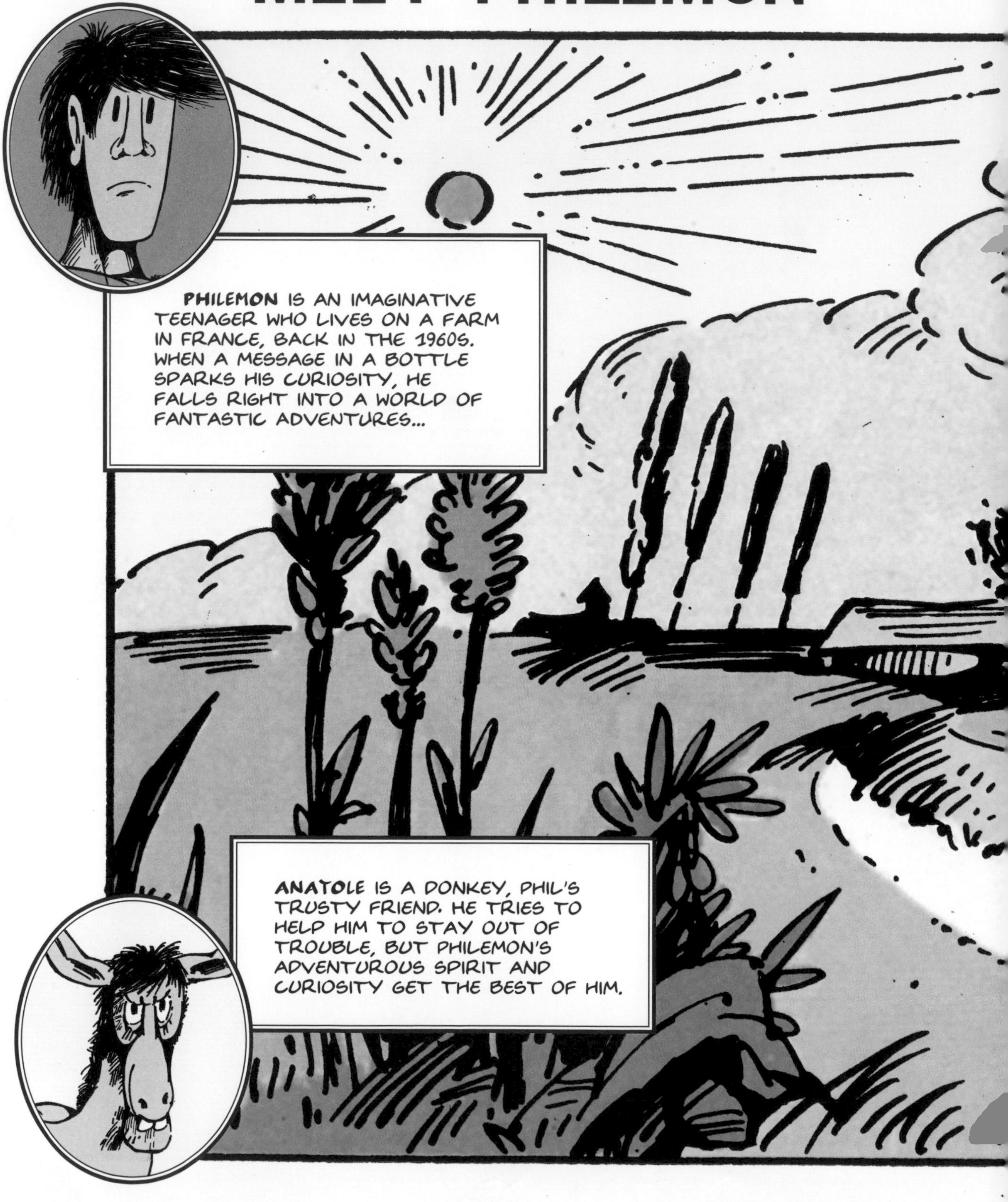
PHILEMON IS AN IMAGINATIVE TEENAGER WHO LIVES ON A FARM IN FRANCE, BACK IN THE 1960S. WHEN A MESSAGE IN A BOTTLE SPARKS HIS CURIOSITY, HE FALLS RIGHT INTO A WORLD OF FANTASTIC ADVENTURES...
ANATOLE IS A DONKEY, PHIL'S TRUSTY FRIEND. HE TRIES TO HELP HIM TO STAY OUT OF TROUBLE, BUT PHILEMON'S ADVENTUROUS SPIRIT AND CURIOSITY GET THE BEST OF HIM.

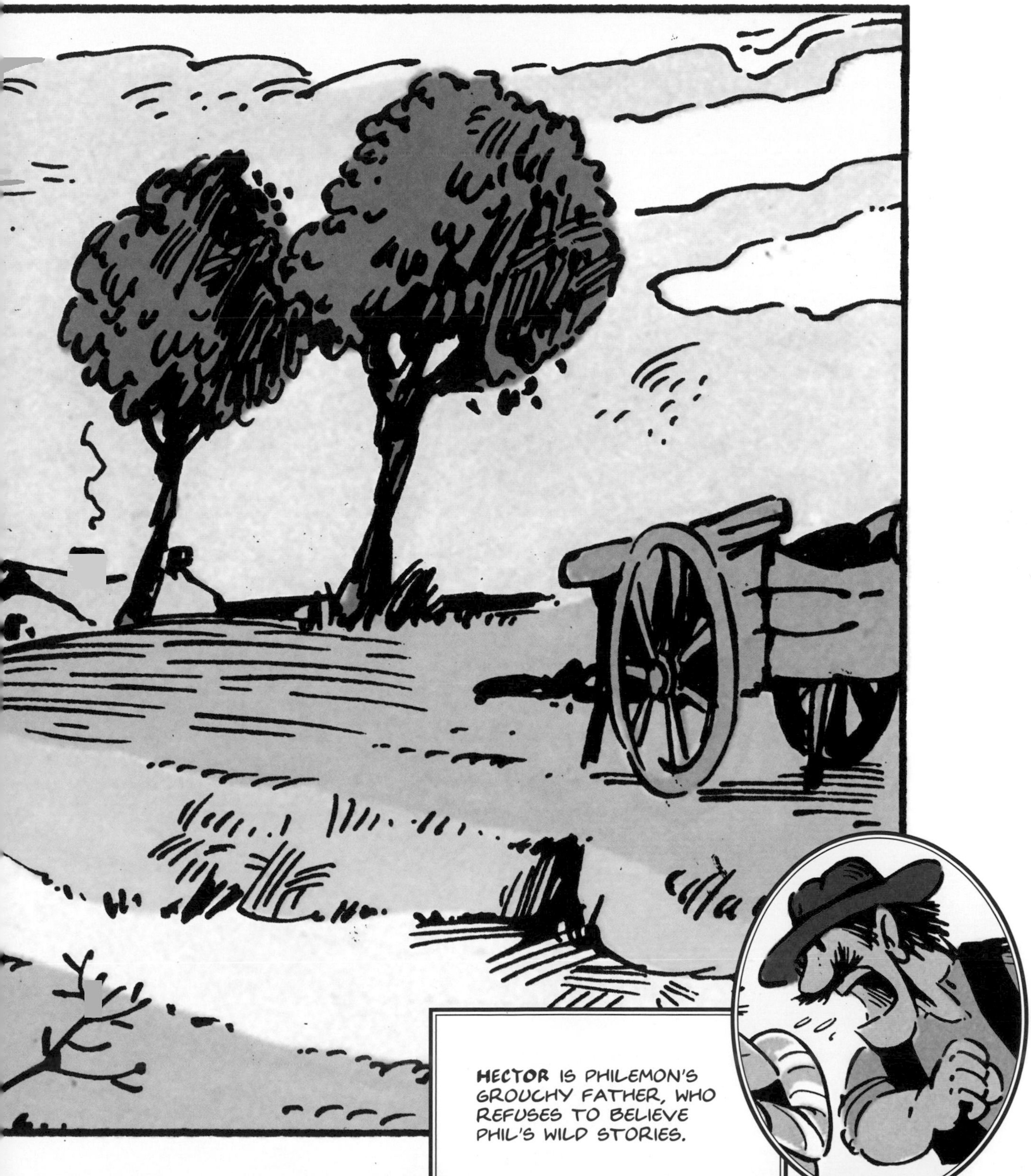

HECTOR IS PHILEMON'S GROUCHY FATHER, WHO REFUSES TO BELIEVE PHIL'S WILD STORIES.

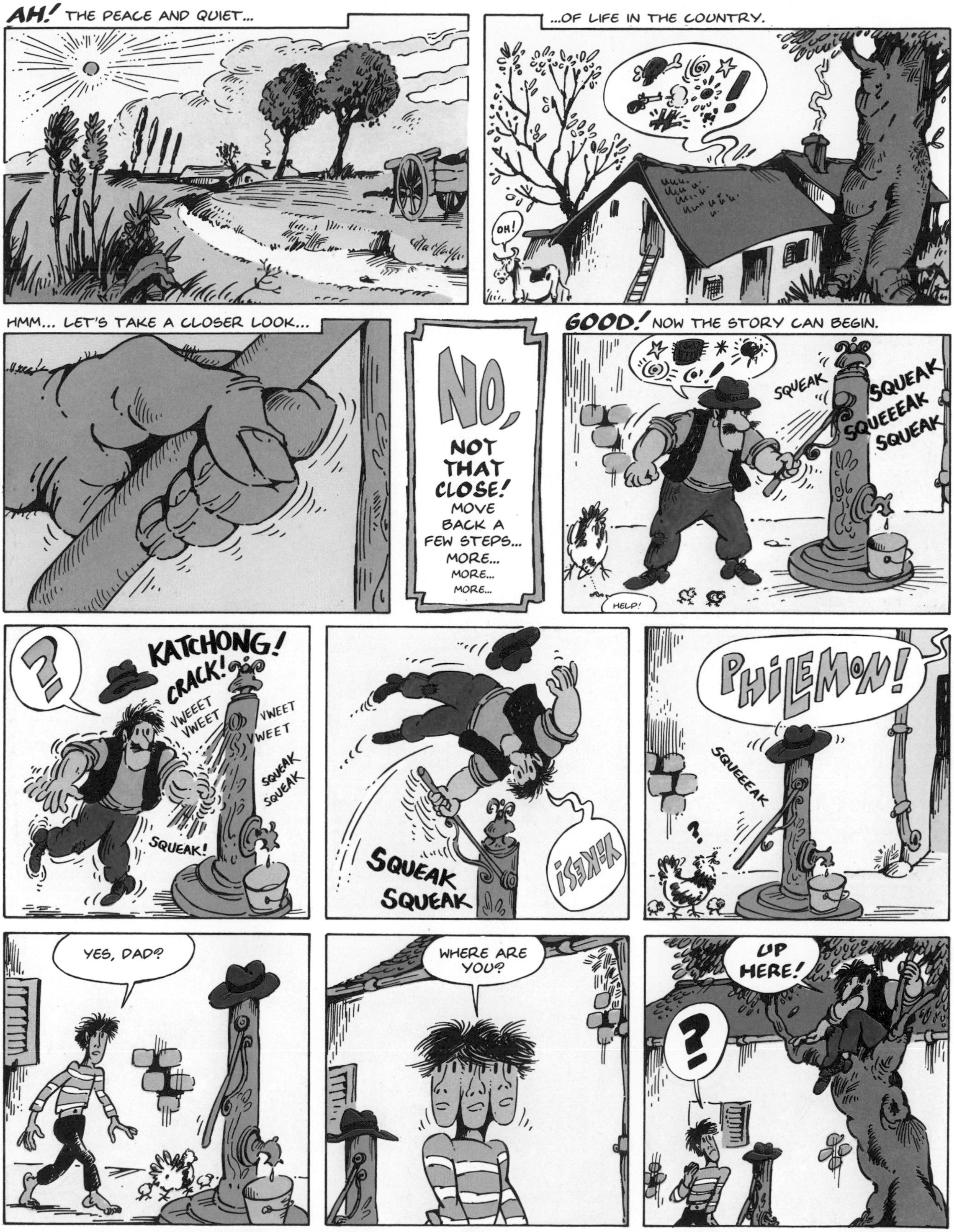
AH! THE PEACE AND QUIET...
...OF LIFE IN THE COUNTRY.
OH!
HMM... LET'S TAKE A CLOSER LOOK...
NO, NOT THAT CLOSE! MOVE BACK A FEW STEPS... MORE... MORE... MORE...
GOOD! NOW THE STORY CAN BEGIN.
SQUEAK
SQUEAK SQUEEEAK SQUEAK
HELP!
?
KATCHONG! CRACK!
VWEEET VWEET
VWEET VWEET
SQUEAK SQUEAK
SQUEAK!
SQUEAK SQUEAK
YIKES!
PHILEMON!
SQUEEEAK
?
YES, DAD?
WHERE ARE YOU?
UP HERE!
?

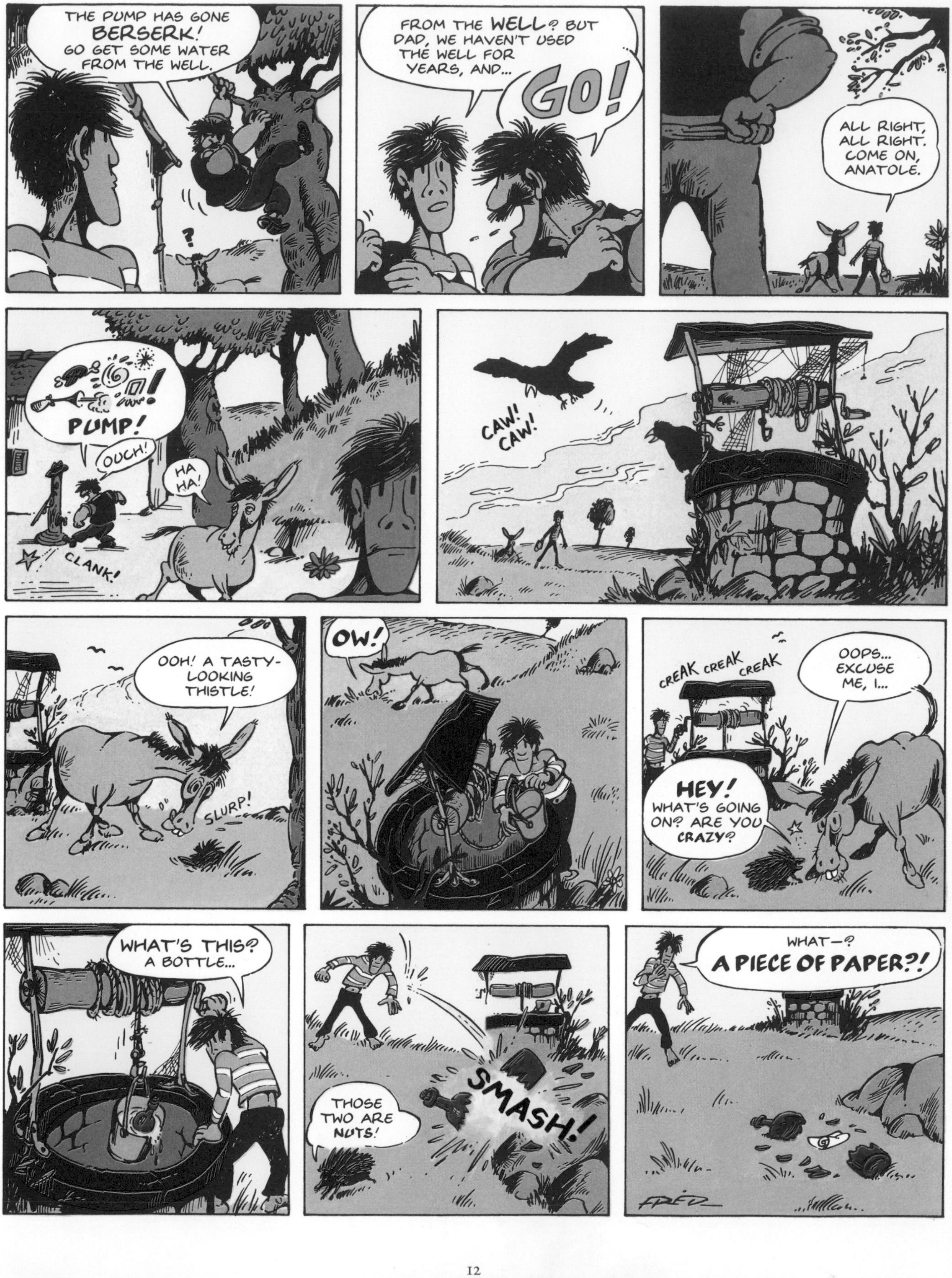
THE PUMP HAS GONE BERSERK! GO GET SOME WATER FROM THE WELL.
?
FROM THE WELL? BUT DAD, WE HAVEN'T USED THE WELL FOR YEARS, AND...
GO!
ALL RIGHT, ALL RIGHT. COME ON, ANATOLE.
PUMP!
OUCH!
HA HA!
CLANK!
CAW! CAW!
OOH! A TASTY-LOOKING THISTLE!
SLURP!
OW!
CREAK CREAK CREAK
OOPS... EXCUSE ME, I...
HEY! WHAT'S GOING ON? ARE YOU CRAZY?
WHAT'S THIS? A BOTTLE...
SMASH!
THOSE TWO ARE NUTS!
WHAT—? A PIECE OF PAPER?!
FRED

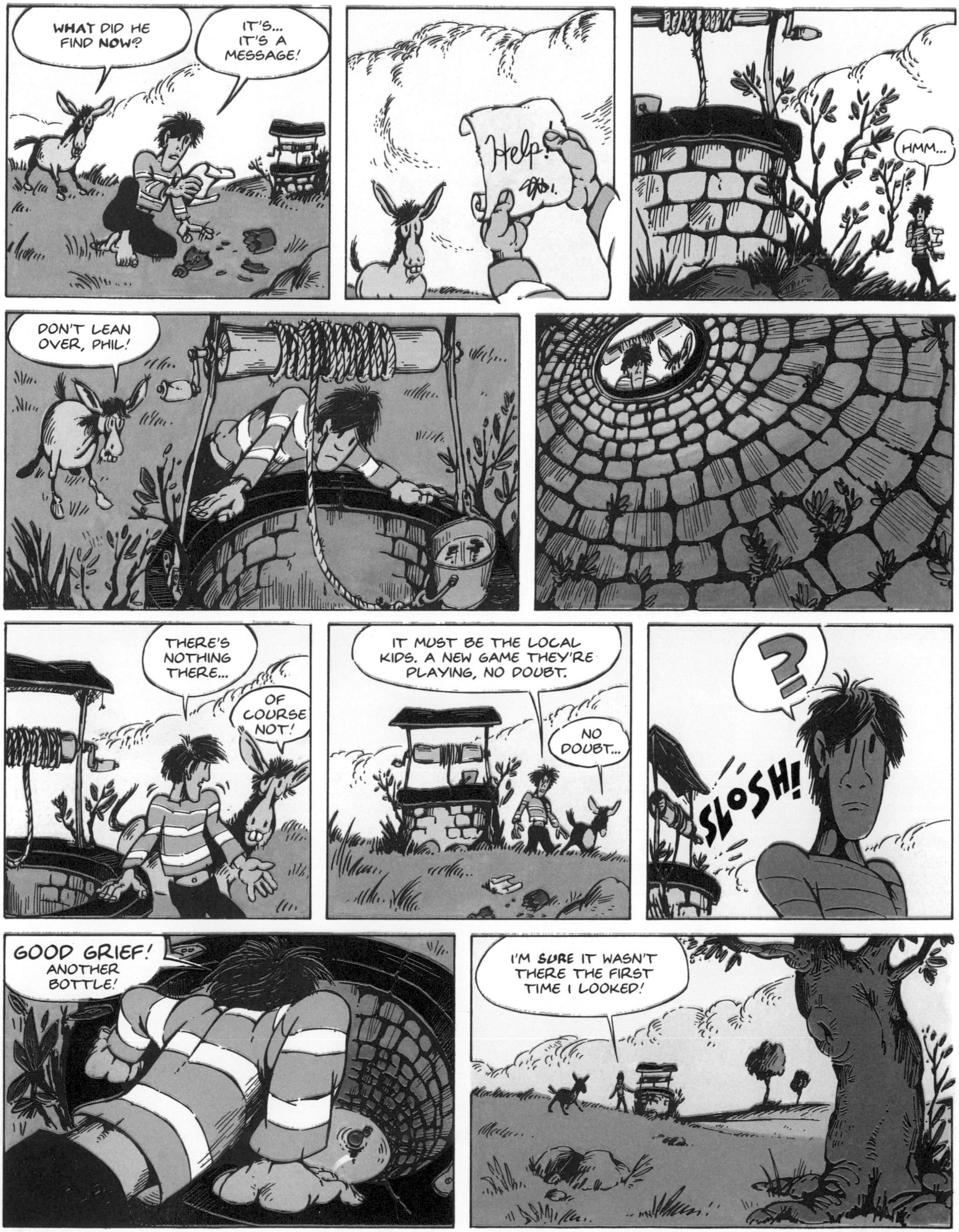
WHAT DID HE FIND NOW?
IT'S... IT'S A MESSAGE!
Help!
HMM...
DON'T LEAN OVER, PHIL!
THERE'S NOTHING THERE...
OF COURSE NOT!
IT MUST BE THE LOCAL KIDS. A NEW GAME THEY'RE PLAYING, NO DOUBT.
NO DOUBT...
?
SLOSH!
GOOD GRIEF! ANOTHER BOTTLE!
I'M SURE IT WASN'T THERE THE FIRST TIME I LOOKED!

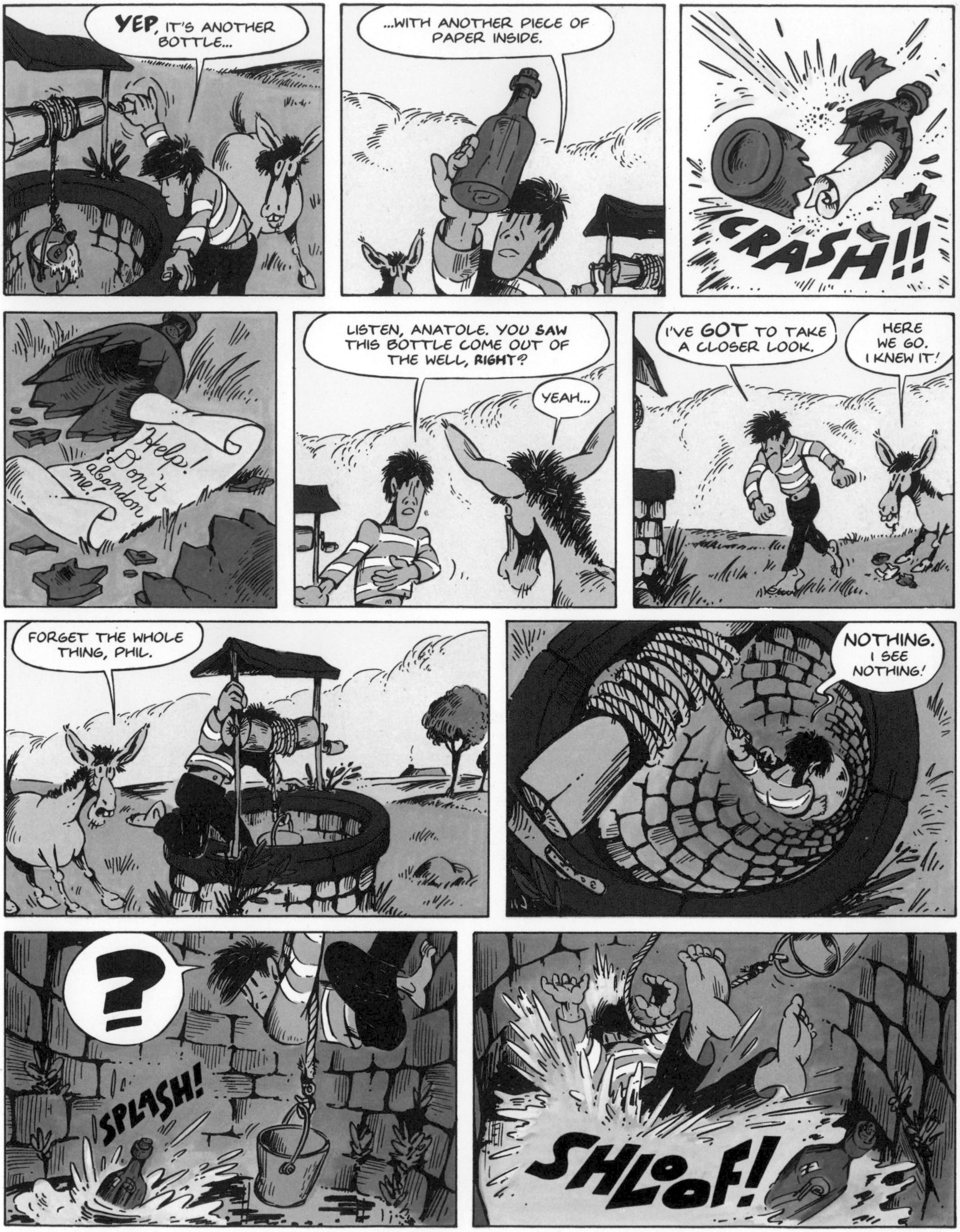
YEP, IT'S ANOTHER BOTTLE...
...WITH ANOTHER PIECE OF PAPER INSIDE.
CRASH!!
Help! Don't abandon me!
LISTEN, ANATOLE. YOU SAW THIS BOTTLE COME OUT OF THE WELL, RIGHT?
YEAH...
I'VE GOT TO TAKE A CLOSER LOOK.
HERE WE GO. I KNEW IT!
FORGET THE WHOLE THING, PHIL.
NOTHING. I SEE NOTHING!
?
SPLASH!
SHLOOF!

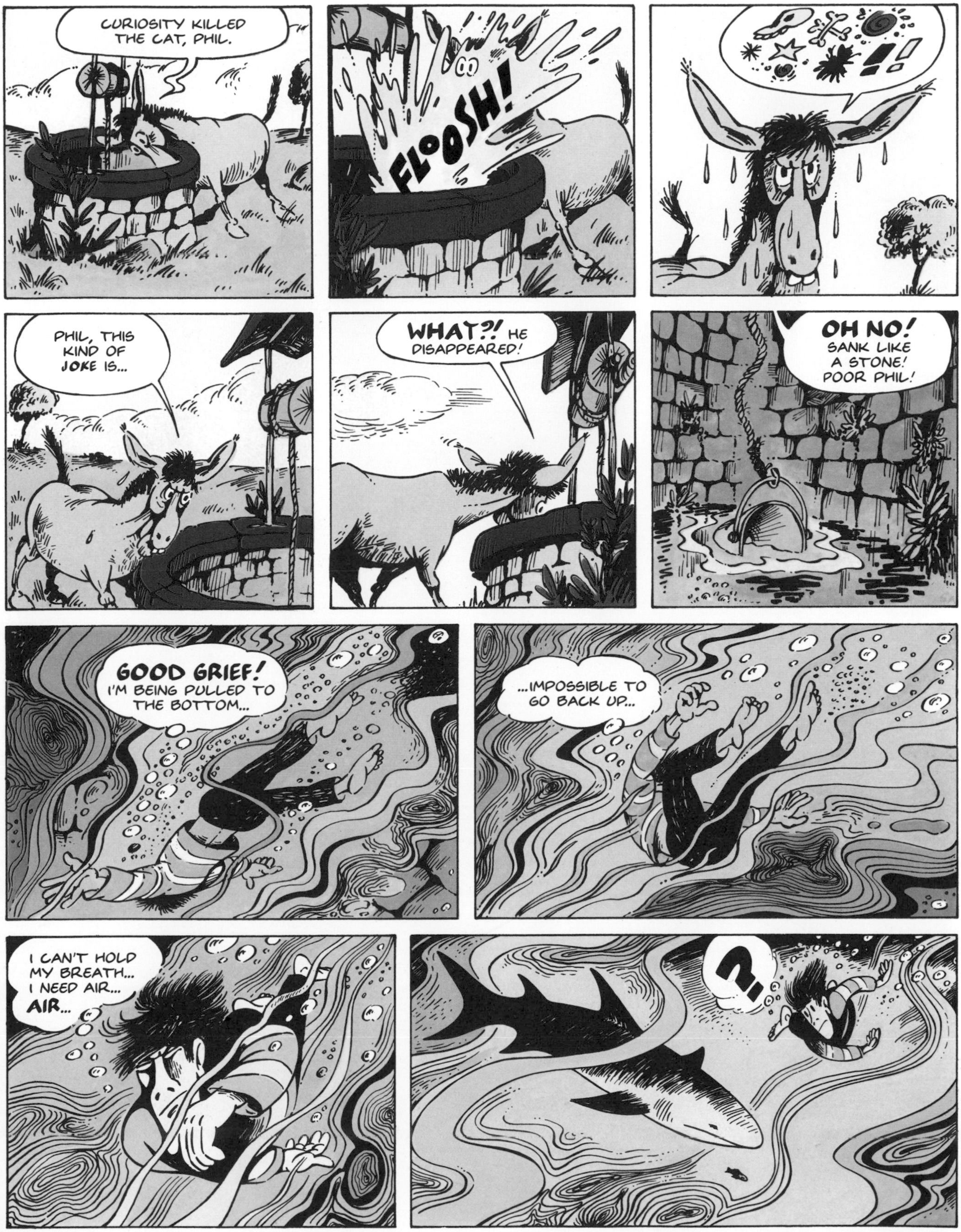
CURIOSITY KILLED THE CAT, PHIL.
FLOOSH!
PHIL, THIS KIND OF JOKE IS...
WHAT?! HE DISAPPEARED!
OH NO! SANK LIKE A STONE! POOR PHIL!
GOOD GRIEF! I'M BEING PULLED TO THE BOTTOM...
...IMPOSSIBLE TO GO BACK UP...
I CAN'T HOLD MY BREATH... I NEED AIR... AIR...
?!

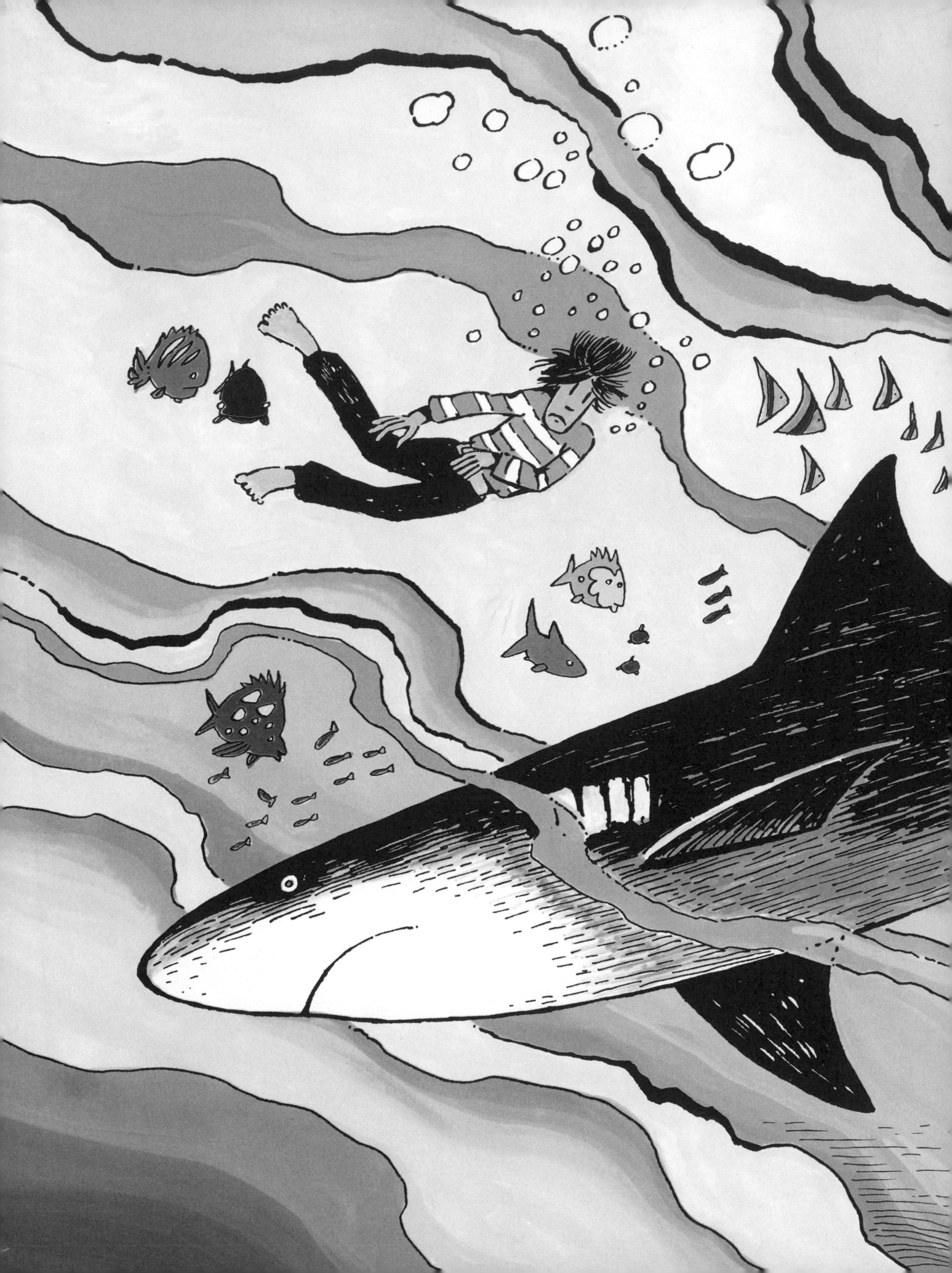

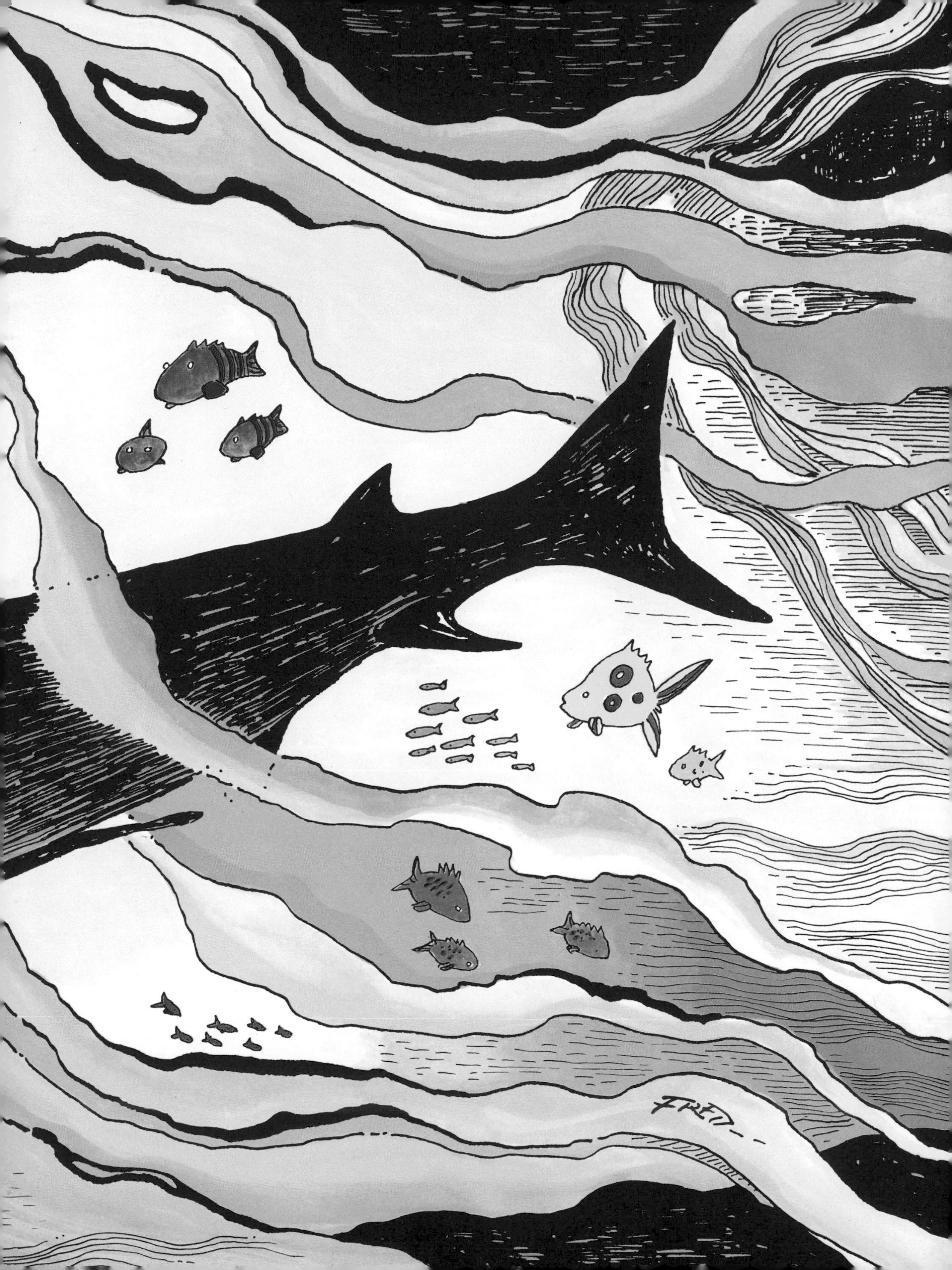
FRED

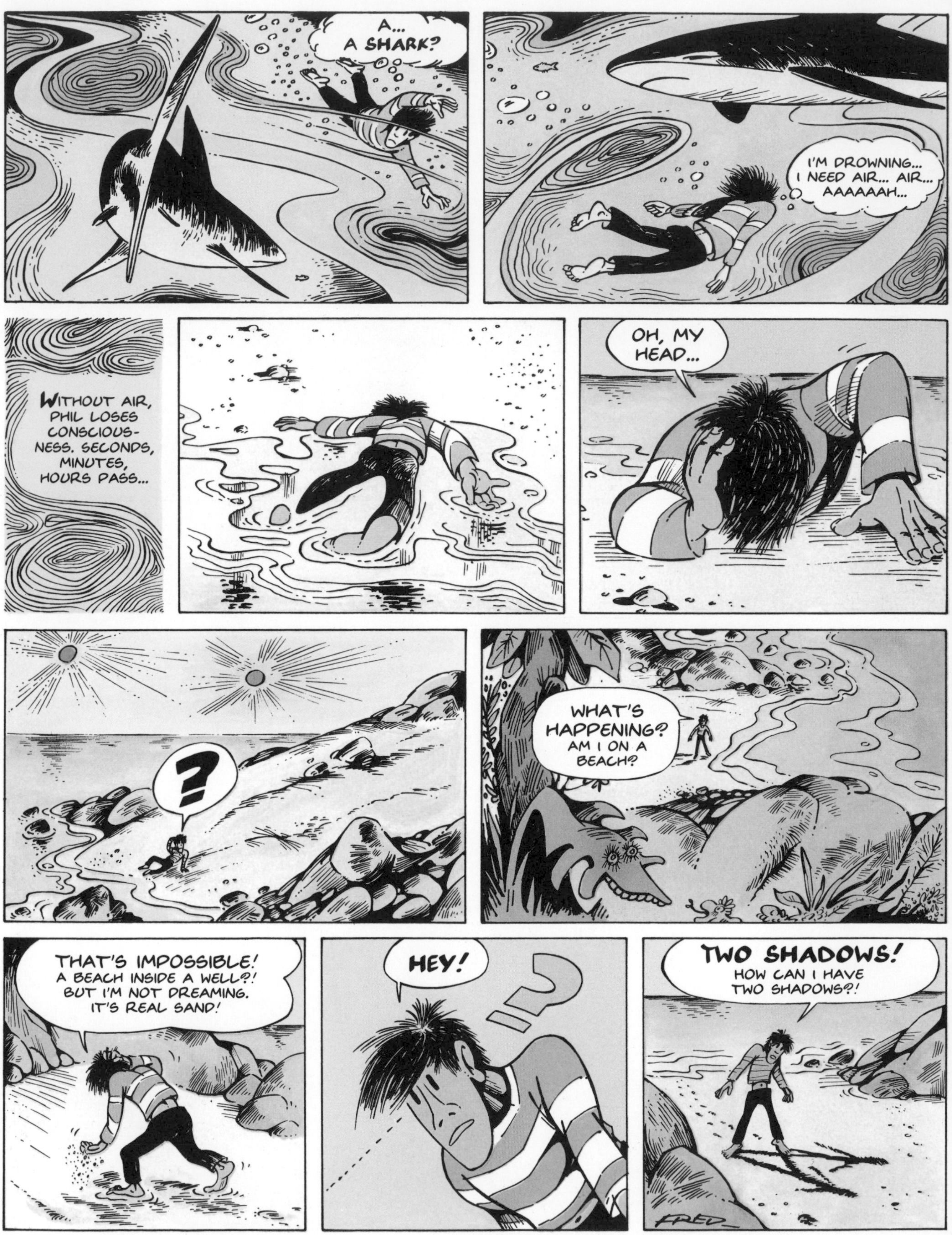
A... A SHARK?
I'M DROWNING... I NEED AIR... AIR... AAAAAAH...
WITHOUT AIR, PHIL LOSES CONSCIOUS-NESS. SECONDS, MINUTES, HOURS PASS...
OH, MY HEAD...
?
WHAT'S HAPPENING? AM I ON A BEACH?
THAT'S IMPOSSIBLE! A BEACH INSIDE A WELL?! BUT I'M NOT DREAMING. IT'S REAL SAND!
HEY!
TWO SHADOWS! HOW CAN I HAVE TWO SHADOWS?!
FRED

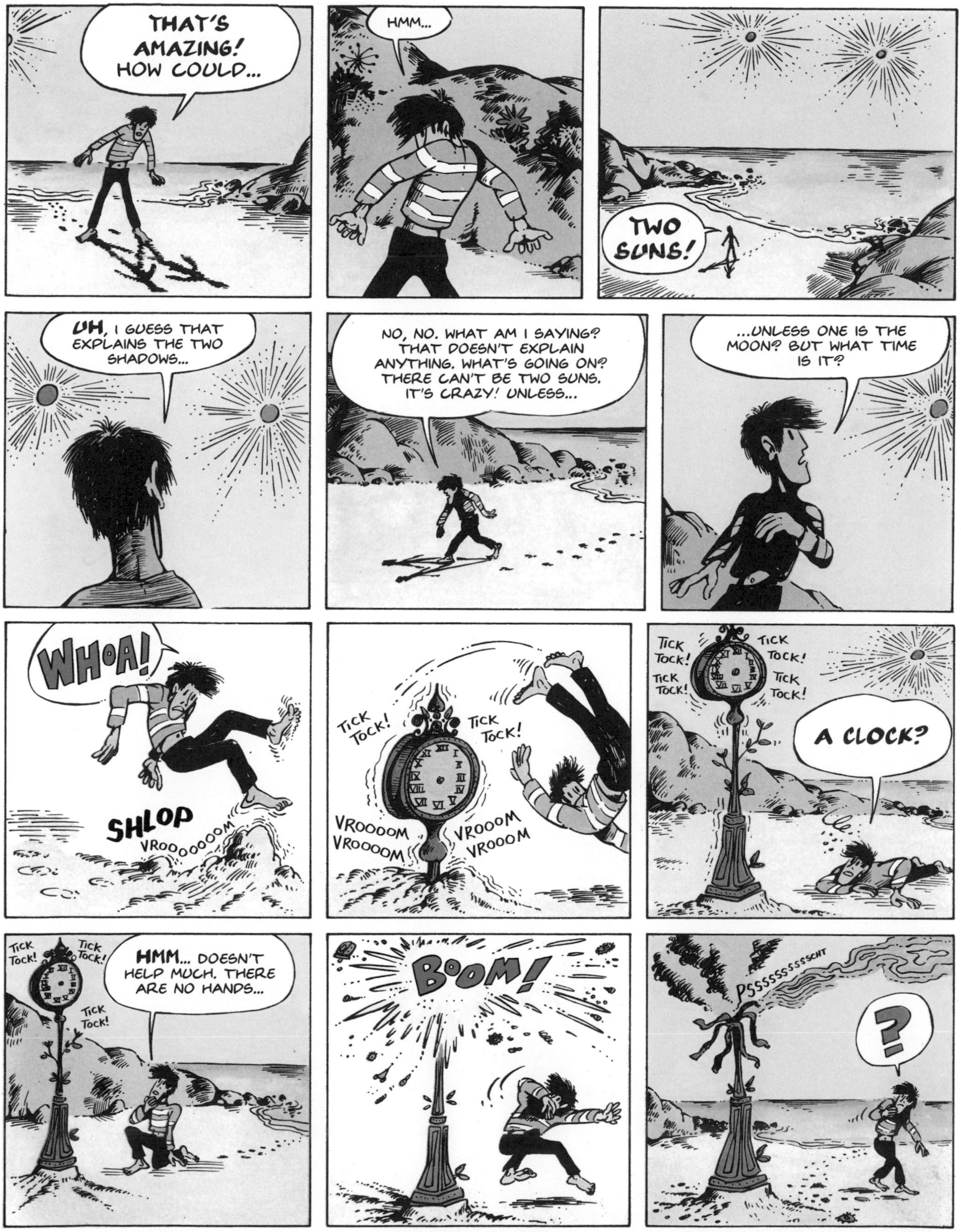
THAT'S AMAZING! HOW COULD...
HMM...
TWO SUNS!
UH, I GUESS THAT EXPLAINS THE TWO SHADOWS...
NO, NO. WHAT AM I SAYING? THAT DOESN'T EXPLAIN ANYTHING. WHAT'S GOING ON? THERE CAN'T BE TWO SUNS. IT'S CRAZY! UNLESS...
...UNLESS ONE IS THE MOON? BUT WHAT TIME IS IT?
WHOA!
SHLOP
VROOOOOOOM
TICK TOCK!
TICK TOCK!
VROOOOM VROOOOM
VROOOM VROOOM
TICK TOCK!
TICK TOCK!
TICK TOCK!
TICK TOCK!
A CLOCK?
TICK TOCK!
TICK TOCK!
TICK TOCK!
HMM... DOESN'T HELP MUCH. THERE ARE NO HANDS...
BOOM!
PSSSSSSSSSSCHT
?

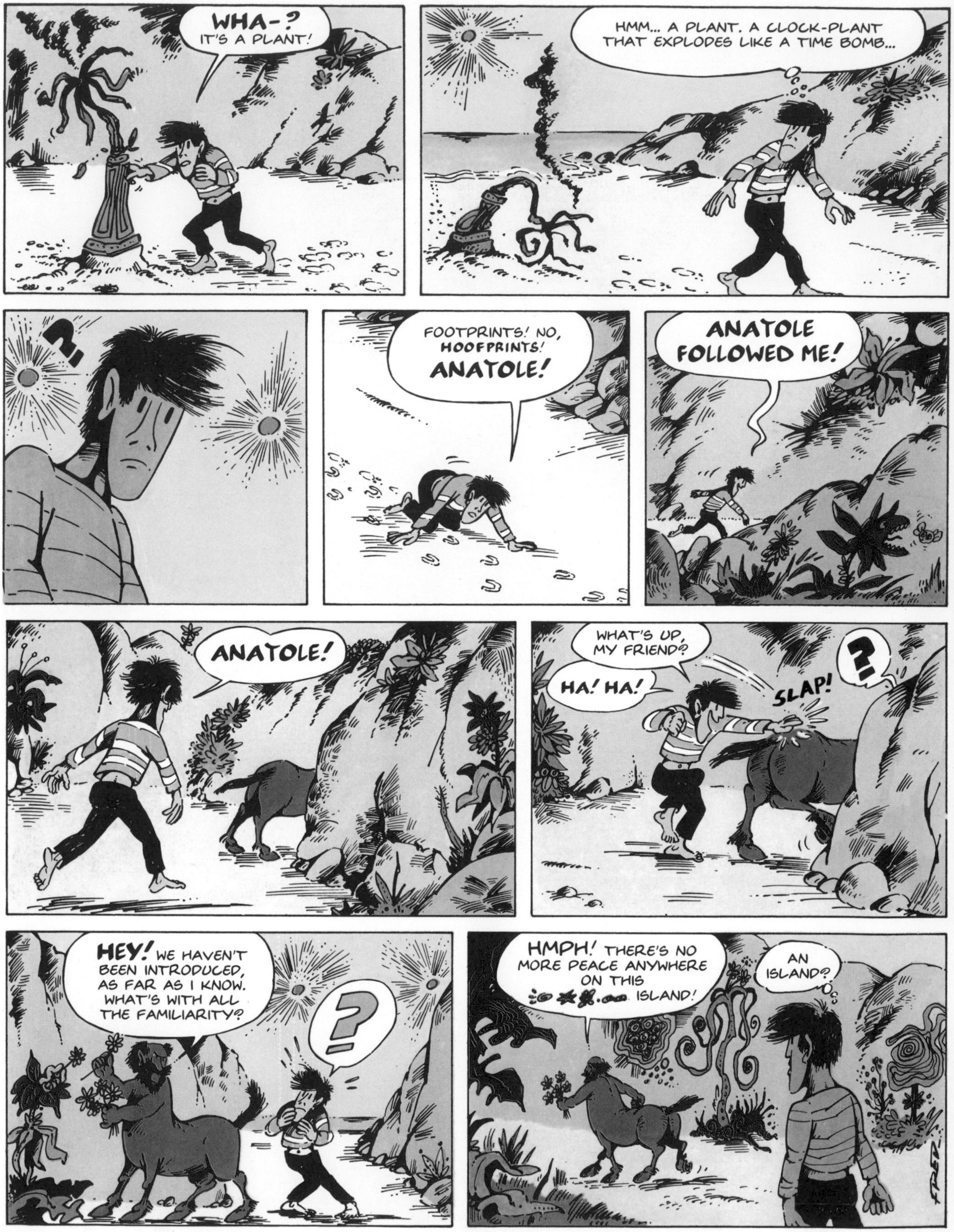
WHA-? IT'S A PLANT!
HMM... A PLANT. A CLOCK-PLANT THAT EXPLODES LIKE A TIME BOMB...
?!
FOOTPRINTS! NO, HOOFPRINTS! ANATOLE!
ANATOLE FOLLOWED ME!
ANATOLE!
WHAT'S UP, MY FRIEND?
HA! HA!
SLAP!
?!
HEY! WE HAVEN'T BEEN INTRODUCED, AS FAR AS I KNOW. WHAT'S WITH ALL THE FAMILIARITY?
?
HMPH! THERE'S NO MORE PEACE ANYWHERE ON THIS ISLAND!
AN ISLAND?
FRED

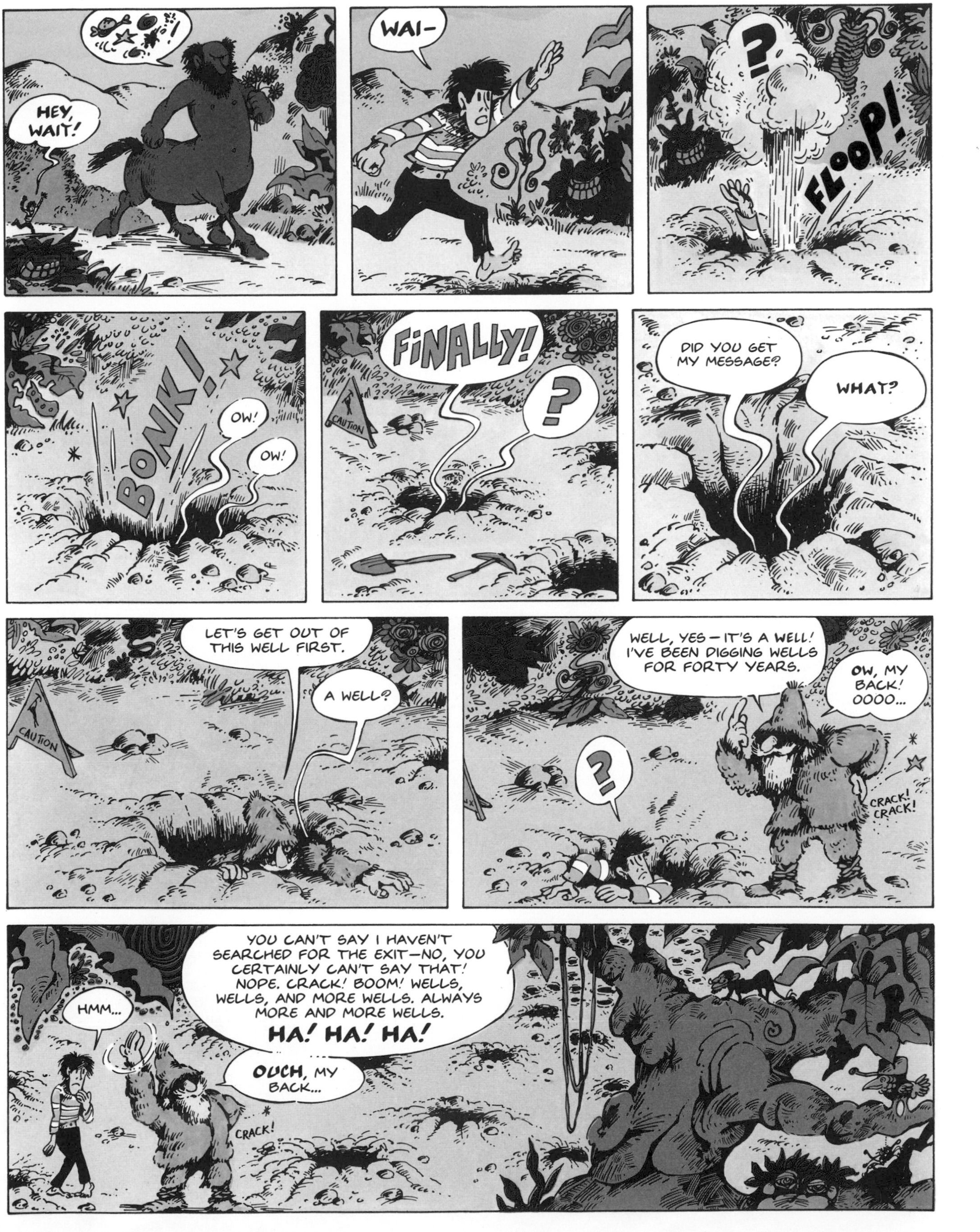
HEY, WAIT!
WAI-
?
FLOOP!
BONK!
OW!
OW!
FINALLY!
?
DID YOU GET MY MESSAGE?
WHAT?
LET'S GET OUT OF THIS WELL FIRST.
A WELL?
WELL, YES—IT'S A WELL! I'VE BEEN DIGGING WELLS FOR FORTY YEARS.
OW, MY BACK! OOOO...
?
CRACK! CRACK!
HMM...
YOU CAN'T SAY I HAVEN'T SEARCHED FOR THE EXIT—NO, YOU CERTAINLY CAN'T SAY THAT! NOPE. CRACK! BOOM! WELLS, WELLS, AND MORE WELLS. ALWAYS MORE AND MORE WELLS. HA! HA! HA!
OUCH, MY BACK...
CRACK!

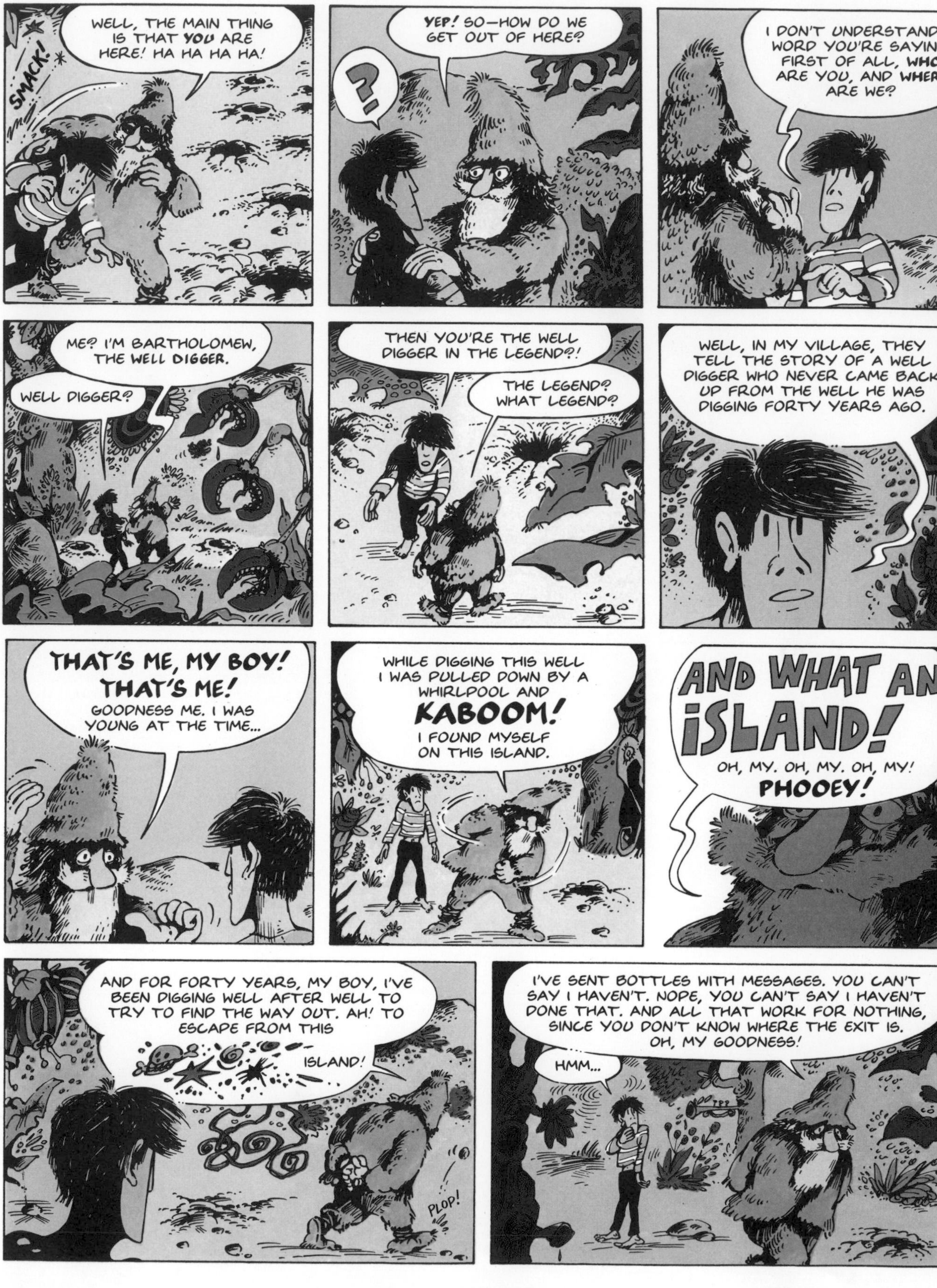
WELL, THE MAIN THING IS THAT YOU ARE HERE! HA HA HA HA!
SMACK!
YEP! SO—HOW DO WE GET OUT OF HERE?
?
I DON'T UNDERSTAND A WORD YOU'RE SAYING. FIRST OF ALL, WHO ARE YOU, AND WHERE ARE WE?
ME? I'M BARTHOLOMEW, THE WELL DIGGER.
WELL DIGGER?
THEN YOU'RE THE WELL DIGGER IN THE LEGEND?!
THE LEGEND? WHAT LEGEND?
WELL, IN MY VILLAGE, THEY TELL THE STORY OF A WELL DIGGER WHO NEVER CAME BACK UP FROM THE WELL HE WAS DIGGING FORTY YEARS AGO.
THAT'S ME, MY BOY! THAT'S ME! GOODNESS ME. I WAS YOUNG AT THE TIME...
WHILE DIGGING THIS WELL I WAS PULLED DOWN BY A WHIRLPOOL AND KABOOM! I FOUND MYSELF ON THIS ISLAND.
AND WHAT AN ISLAND! OH, MY. OH, MY. OH, MY! PHOOEY!
AND FOR FORTY YEARS, MY BOY, I'VE BEEN DIGGING WELL AFTER WELL TO TRY TO FIND THE WAY OUT. AH! TO ESCAPE FROM THIS ISLAND!
PLOP!
I'VE SENT BOTTLES WITH MESSAGES. YOU CAN'T SAY I HAVEN'T. NOPE, YOU CAN'T SAY I HAVEN'T DONE THAT. AND ALL THAT WORK FOR NOTHING, SINCE YOU DON'T KNOW WHERE THE EXIT IS. OH, MY GOODNESS!
HMM...
FRED

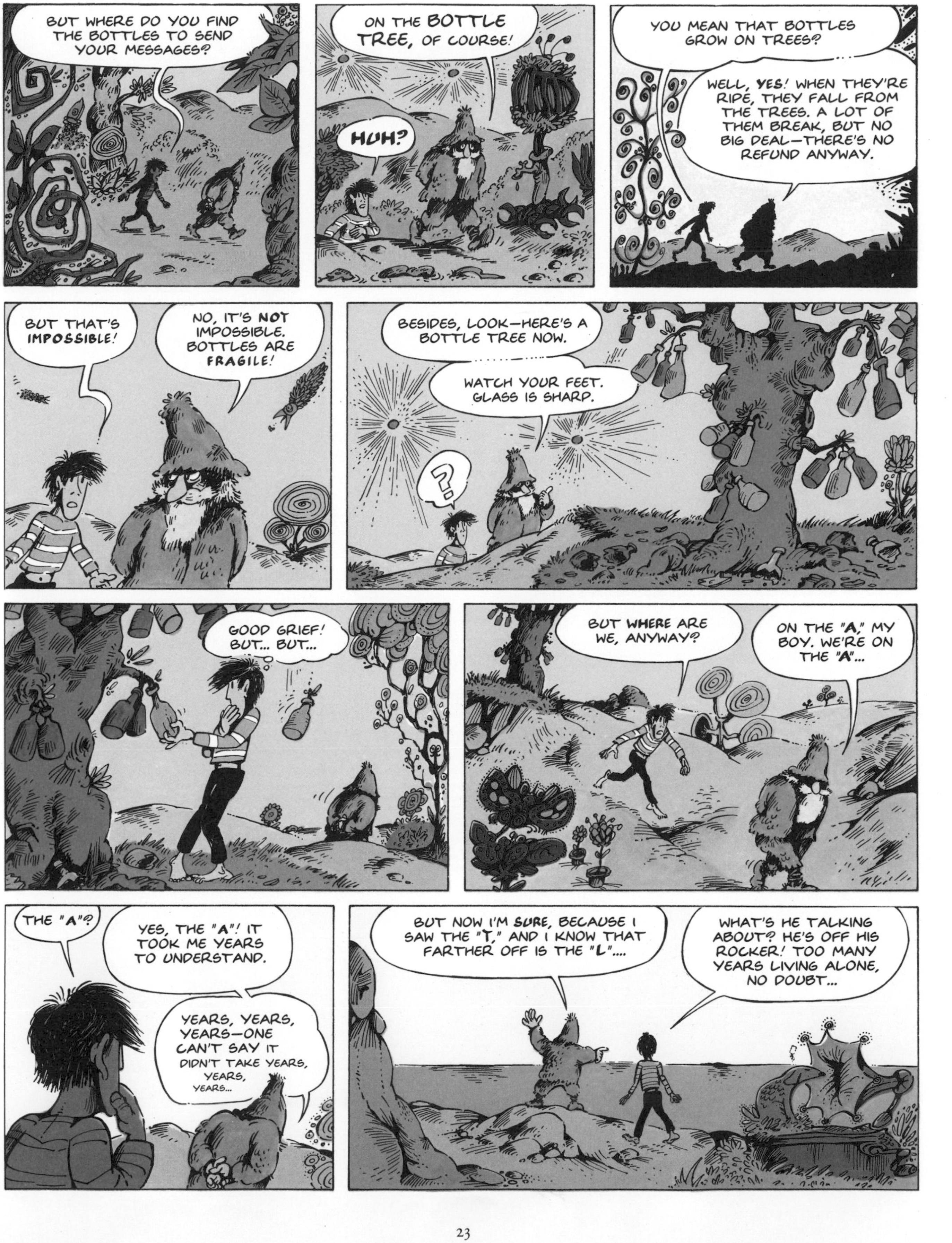

BUT WHERE DO YOU FIND THE BOTTLES TO SEND YOUR MESSAGES?
ON THE BOTTLE TREE, OF COURSE!
HUH?
YOU MEAN THAT BOTTLES GROW ON TREES?
WELL, YES! WHEN THEY'RE RIPE, THEY FALL FROM THE TREES. A LOT OF THEM BREAK, BUT NO BIG DEAL—THERE'S NO REFUND ANYWAY.
BUT THAT'S IMPOSSIBLE!
NO, IT'S NOT IMPOSSIBLE. BOTTLES ARE FRAGILE!
BESIDES, LOOK—HERE'S A BOTTLE TREE NOW.
WATCH YOUR FEET. GLASS IS SHARP.
?
GOOD GRIEF! BUT... BUT...
BUT WHERE ARE WE, ANYWAY?
ON THE "A," MY BOY. WE'RE ON THE "A"...
THE "A"?
YES, THE "A"! IT TOOK ME YEARS TO UNDERSTAND.
YEARS, YEARS, YEARS—ONE CAN'T SAY IT DIDN'T TAKE YEARS, YEARS, YEARS...
BUT NOW I'M SURE, BECAUSE I SAW THE "T," AND I KNOW THAT FARTHER OFF IS THE "L"....
WHAT'S HE TALKING ABOUT? HE'S OFF HIS ROCKER! TOO MANY YEARS LIVING ALONE, NO DOUBT...

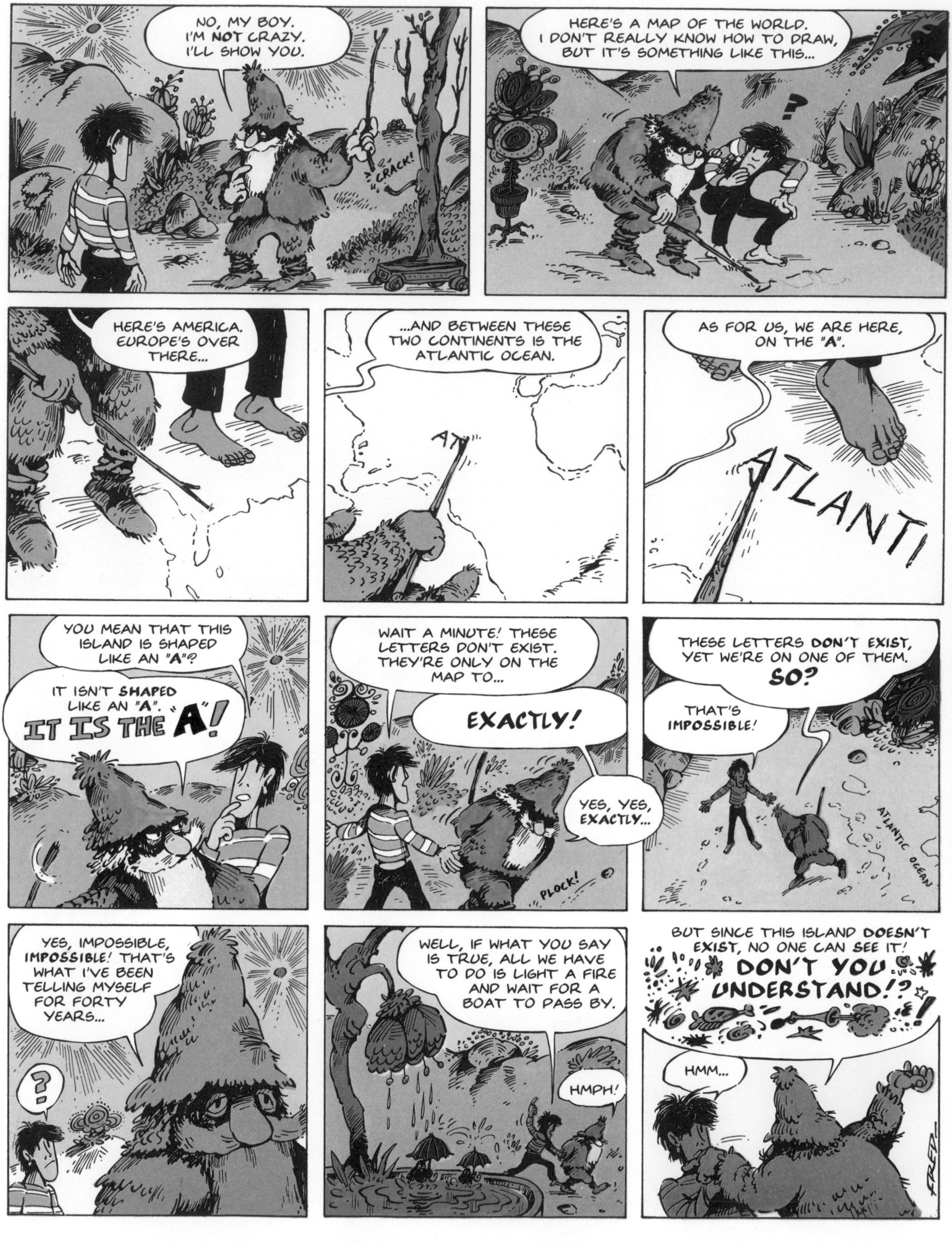

NO, MY BOY. I'M NOT CRAZY. I'LL SHOW YOU.
CRACK!
HERE'S A MAP OF THE WORLD. I DON'T REALLY KNOW HOW TO DRAW, BUT IT'S SOMETHING LIKE THIS...
?
HERE'S AMERICA. EUROPE'S OVER THERE...
...AND BETWEEN THESE TWO CONTINENTS IS THE ATLANTIC OCEAN.
AT
AS FOR US, WE ARE HERE, ON THE "A".
ATLANTI
YOU MEAN THAT THIS ISLAND IS SHAPED LIKE AN "A"?
IT ISN'T SHAPED LIKE AN "A". IT IS THE "A"!
WAIT A MINUTE! THESE LETTERS DON'T EXIST. THEY'RE ONLY ON THE MAP TO...
EXACTLY!
YES, YES, EXACTLY...
PLOCK!
THESE LETTERS DON'T EXIST, YET WE'RE ON ONE OF THEM. SO?
THAT'S IMPOSSIBLE!
ATLANTIC OCEAN
YES, IMPOSSIBLE, IMPOSSIBLE! THAT'S WHAT I'VE BEEN TELLING MYSELF FOR FORTY YEARS...
?
WELL, IF WHAT YOU SAY IS TRUE, ALL WE HAVE TO DO IS LIGHT A FIRE AND WAIT FOR A BOAT TO PASS BY.
HMPH!
BUT SINCE THIS ISLAND DOESN'T EXIST, NO ONE CAN SEE IT! DON'T YOU UNDERSTAND!?!
HMM...
FRED

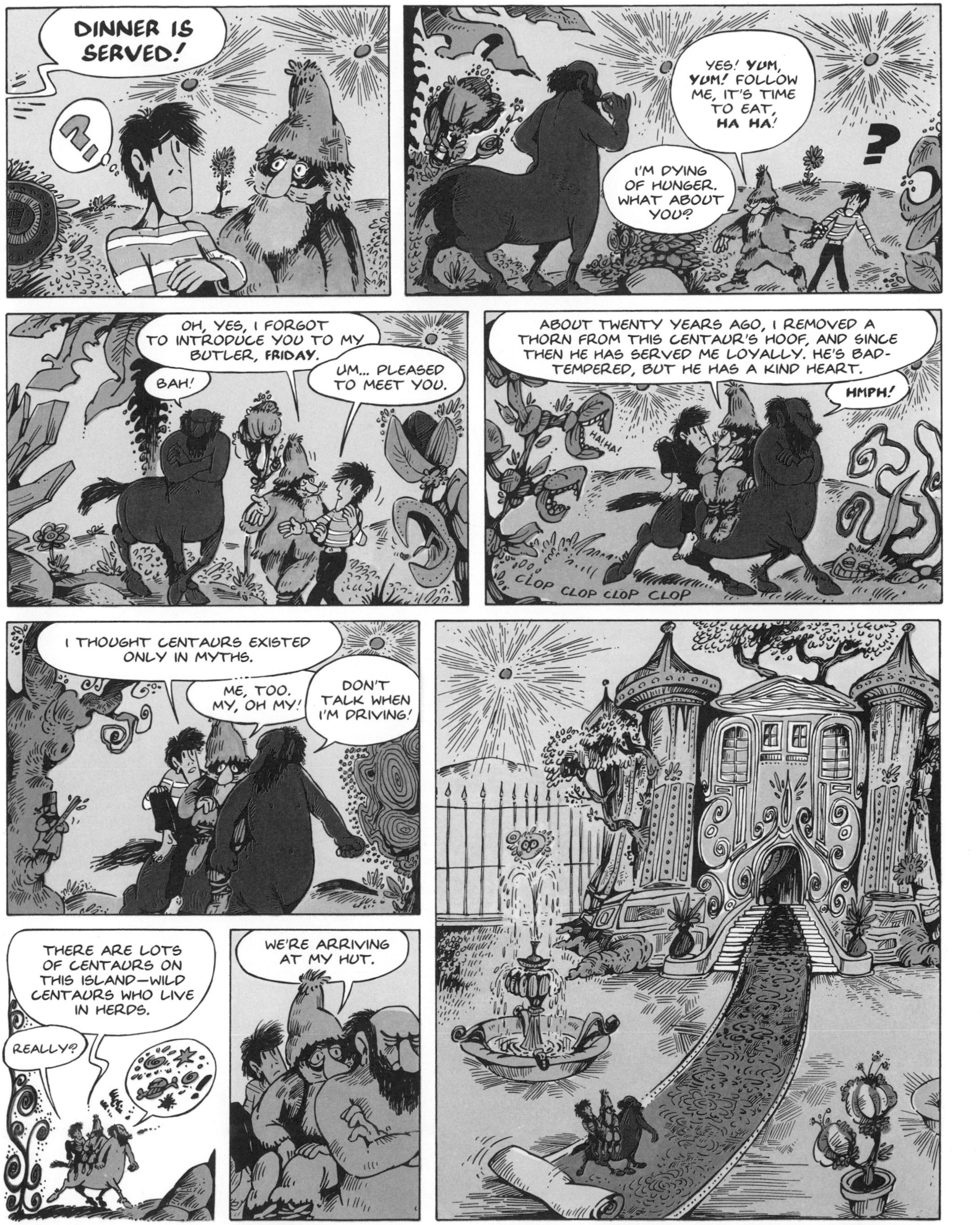
DINNER IS SERVED!
?!
YES! YUM, YUM! FOLLOW ME, IT'S TIME TO EAT, HA HA!
I'M DYING OF HUNGER. WHAT ABOUT YOU?
?
OH, YES, I FORGOT TO INTRODUCE YOU TO MY BUTLER, FRIDAY.
BAH!
UM... PLEASED TO MEET YOU.
ABOUT TWENTY YEARS AGO, I REMOVED A THORN FROM THIS CENTAUR'S HOOF, AND SINCE THEN HE HAS SERVED ME LOYALLY. HE'S BAD-TEMPERED, BUT HE HAS A KIND HEART.
HMPH!
HA!HA!
CLOP CLOP CLOP CLOP
I THOUGHT CENTAURS EXISTED ONLY IN MYTHS.
ME, TOO. MY, OH MY!
DON'T TALK WHEN I'M DRIVING!
THERE ARE LOTS OF CENTAURS ON THIS ISLAND—WILD CENTAURS WHO LIVE IN HERDS.
REALLY?
WE'RE ARRIVING AT MY HUT.

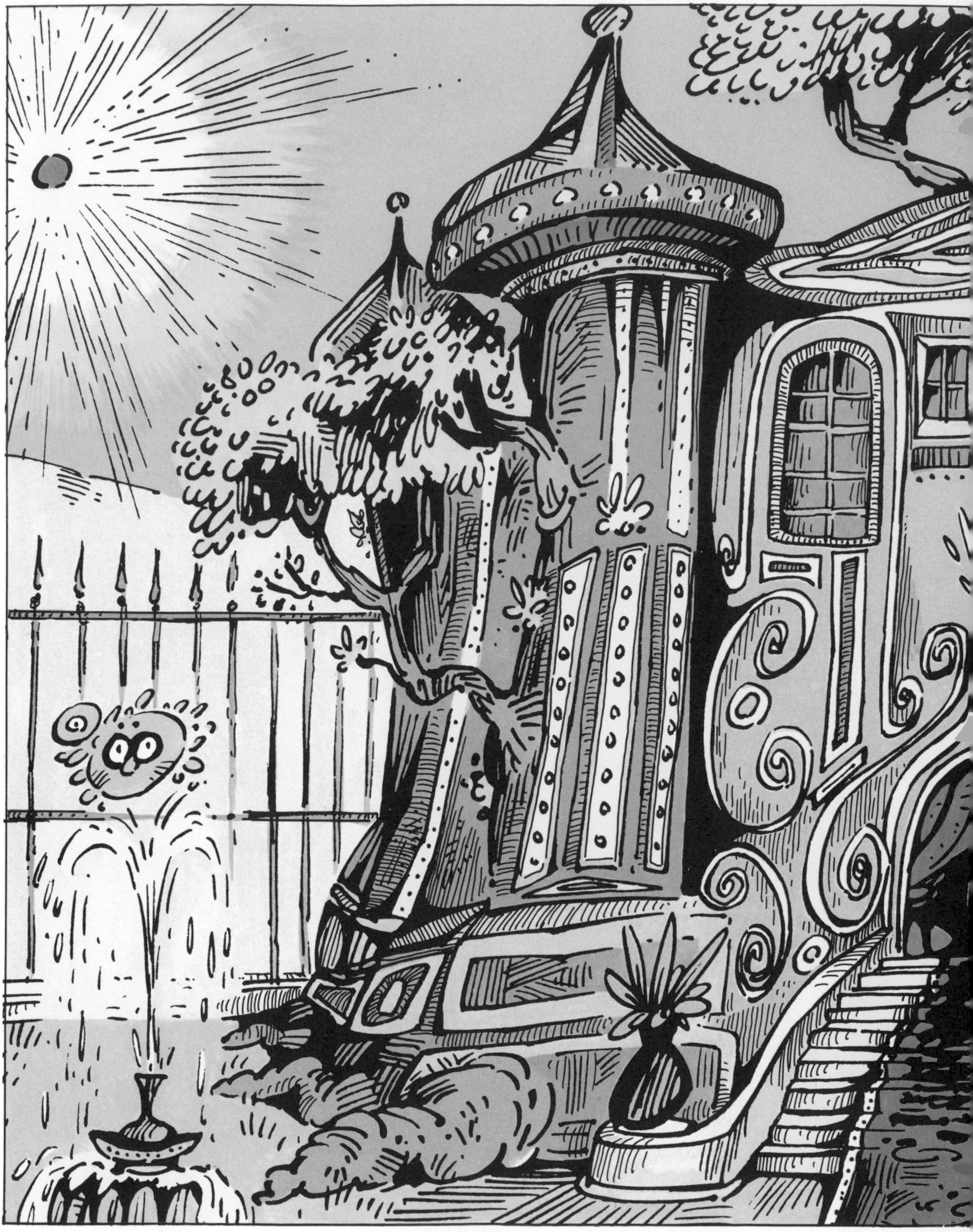

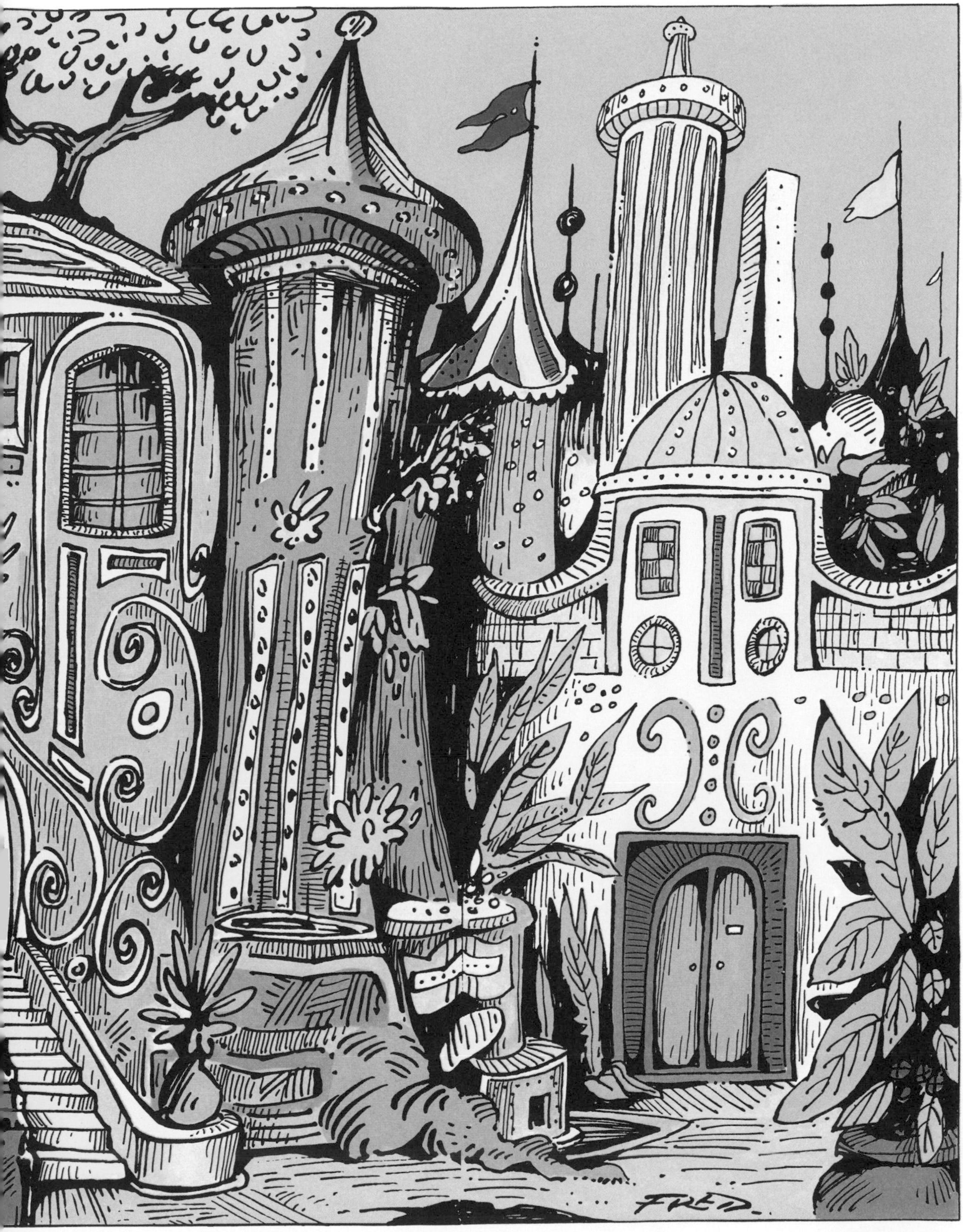
FRED

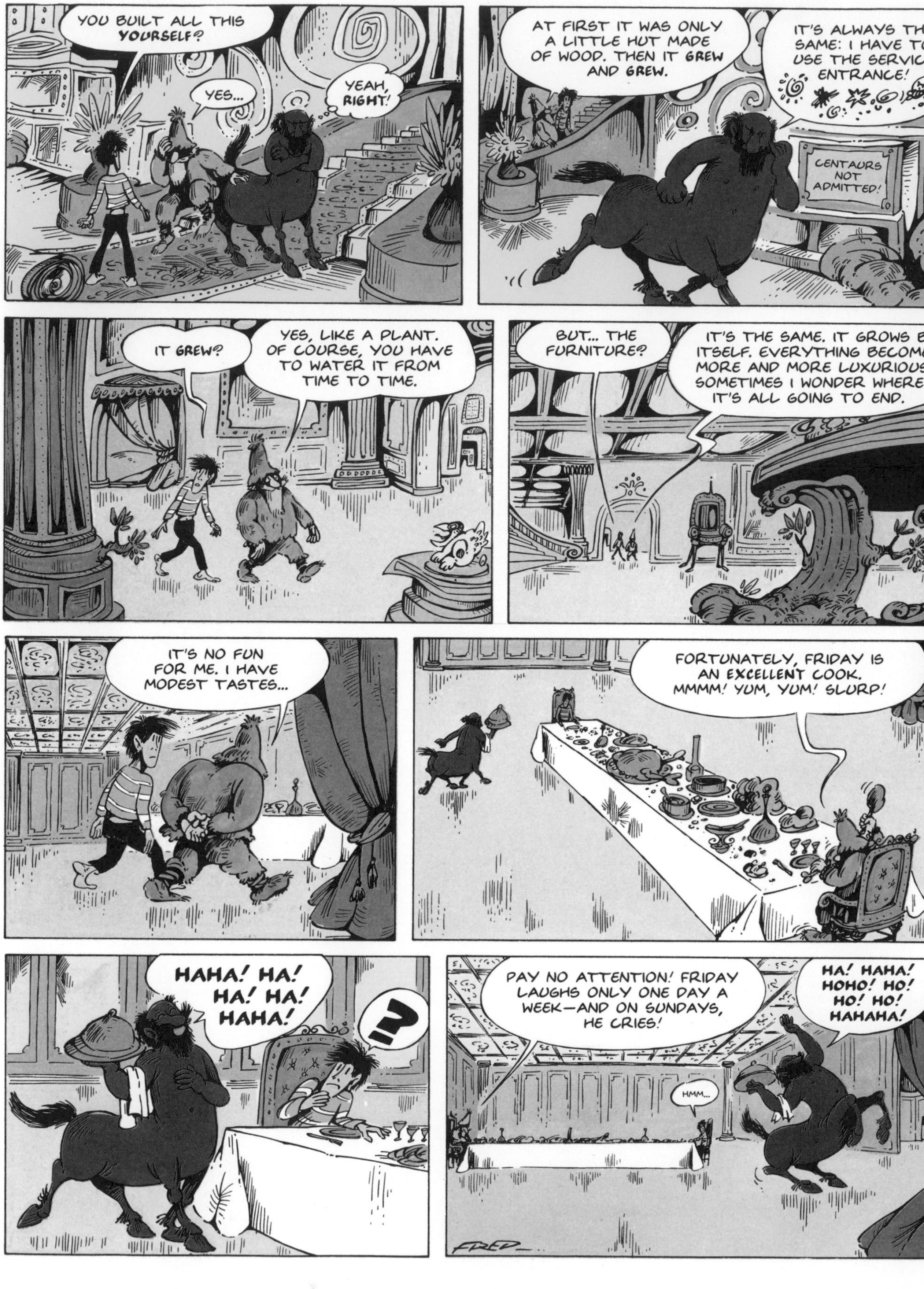

YOU BUILT ALL THIS YOURSELF?
YES...
YEAH, RIGHT!
AT FIRST IT WAS ONLY A LITTLE HUT MADE OF WOOD. THEN IT GREW AND GREW.
IT'S ALWAYS THE SAME: I HAVE TO USE THE SERVICE ENTRANCE!
CENTAURS NOT ADMITTED!
IT GREW?
YES, LIKE A PLANT. OF COURSE, YOU HAVE TO WATER IT FROM TIME TO TIME.
BUT... THE FURNITURE?
IT'S THE SAME. IT GROWS BY ITSELF. EVERYTHING BECOMES MORE AND MORE LUXURIOUS. SOMETIMES I WONDER WHERE IT'S ALL GOING TO END.
IT'S NO FUN FOR ME. I HAVE MODEST TASTES...
FORTUNATELY, FRIDAY IS AN EXCELLENT COOK. MMMM! YUM, YUM! SLURP!
HAHA! HA! HA! HA! HAHA!
?!
PAY NO ATTENTION! FRIDAY LAUGHS ONLY ONE DAY A WEEK—AND ON SUNDAYS, HE CRIES!
HA! HAHA! HOHO! HO! HO! HO! HAHAHA!
HMM...
FRED

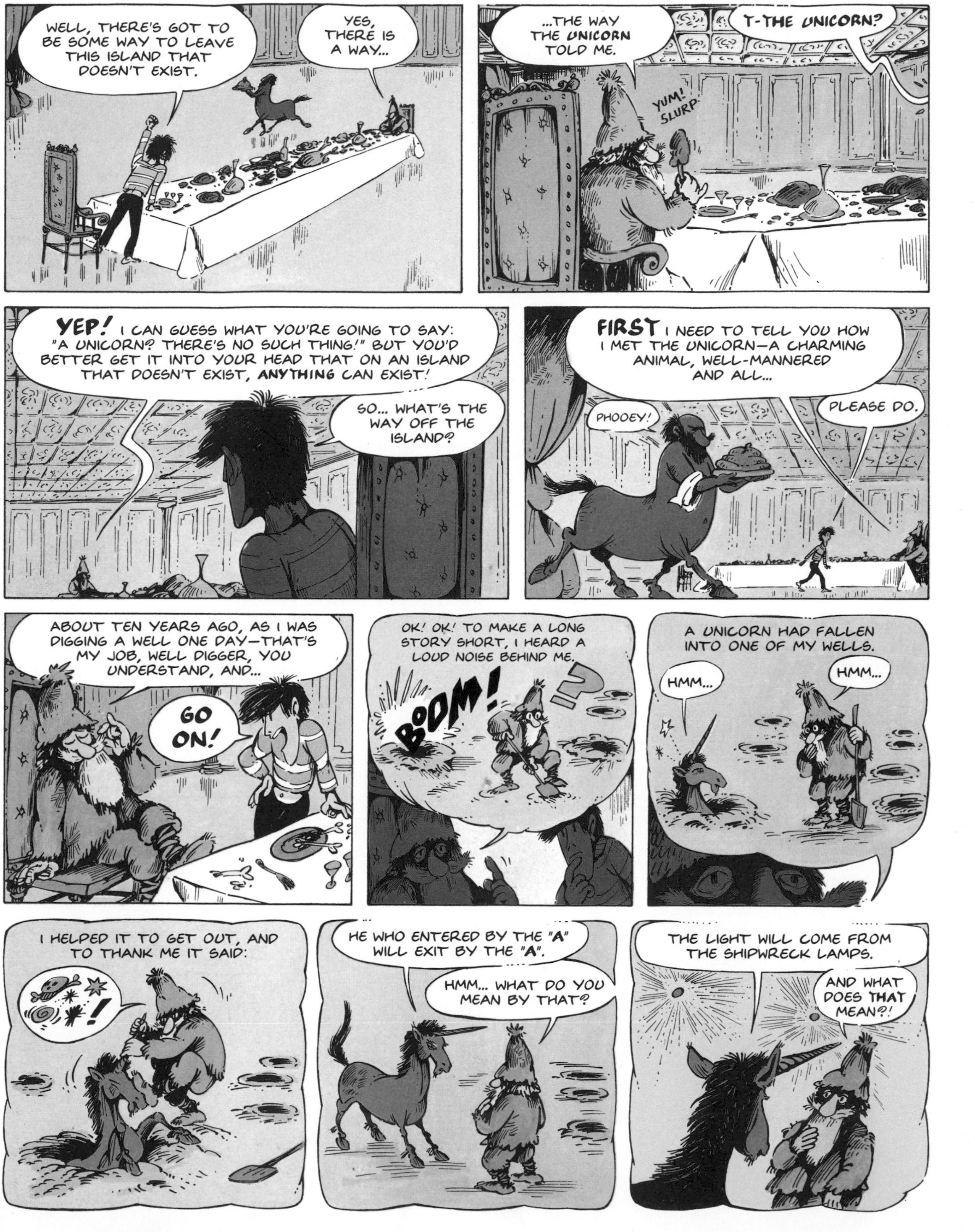

WELL, THERE'S GOT TO BE SOME WAY TO LEAVE THIS ISLAND THAT DOESN'T EXIST.
YES, THERE IS A WAY...
...THE WAY THE UNICORN TOLD ME.
YUM! SLURP
T-THE UNICORN?
YEP! I CAN GUESS WHAT YOU'RE GOING TO SAY: "A UNICORN? THERE'S NO SUCH THING!" BUT YOU'D BETTER GET IT INTO YOUR HEAD THAT ON AN ISLAND THAT DOESN'T EXIST, ANYTHING CAN EXIST!
SO... WHAT'S THE WAY OFF THE ISLAND?
FIRST I NEED TO TELL YOU HOW I MET THE UNICORN—A CHARMING ANIMAL, WELL-MANNERED AND ALL...
PHOOEY!
PLEASE DO.
ABOUT TEN YEARS AGO, AS I WAS DIGGING A WELL ONE DAY—THAT'S MY JOB, WELL DIGGER, YOU UNDERSTAND, AND...
GO ON!
OK! OK! TO MAKE A LONG STORY SHORT, I HEARD A LOUD NOISE BEHIND ME.
BOOM!
?
A UNICORN HAD FALLEN INTO ONE OF MY WELLS.
HMM...
HMM...
I HELPED IT TO GET OUT, AND TO THANK ME IT SAID:
!
HE WHO ENTERED BY THE "A" WILL EXIT BY THE "A".
HMM... WHAT DO YOU MEAN BY THAT?
THE LIGHT WILL COME FROM THE SHIPWRECK LAMPS.
AND WHAT DOES THAT MEAN?!

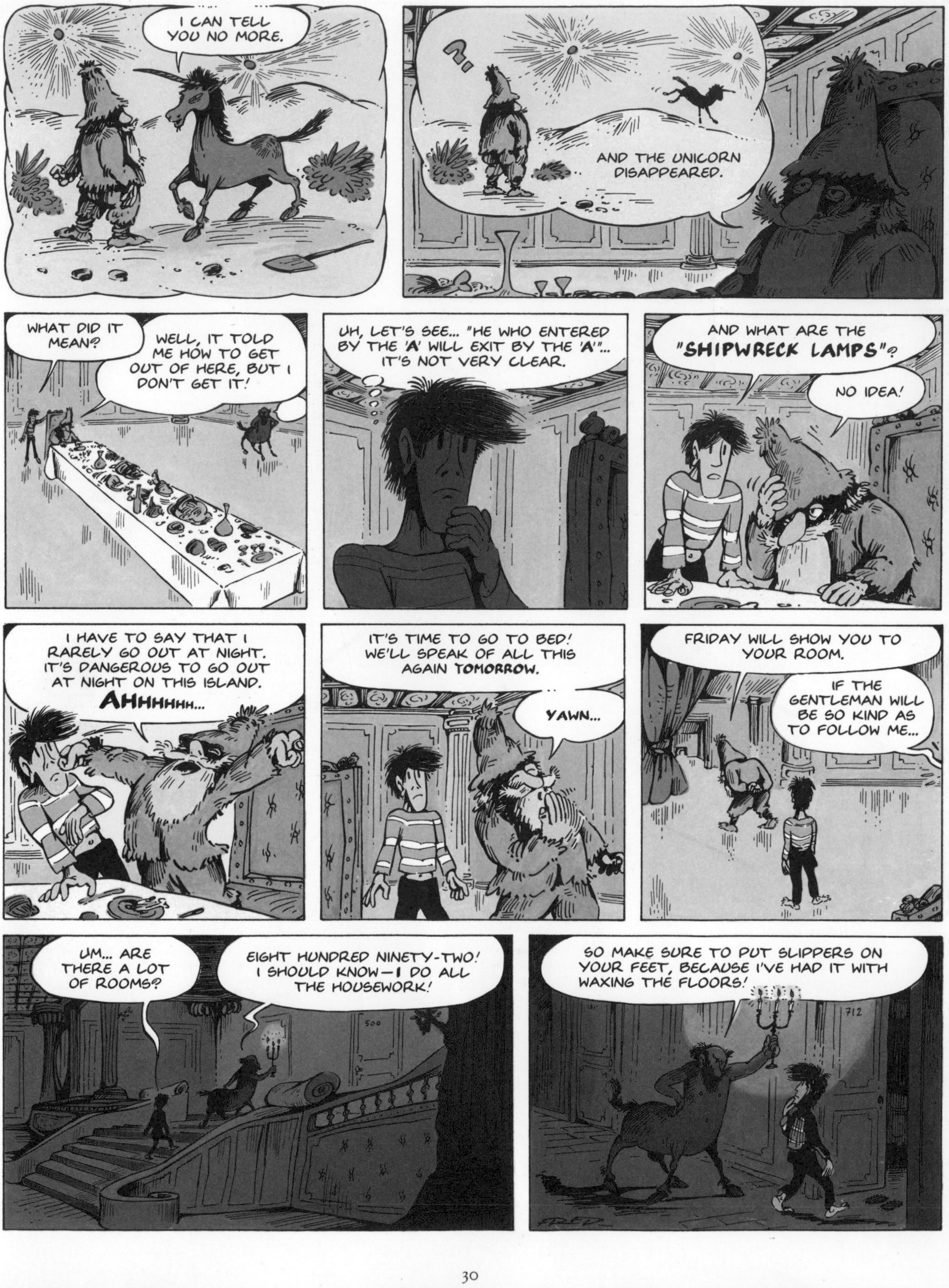

I CAN TELL YOU NO MORE.
AND THE UNICORN DISAPPEARED.
WHAT DID IT MEAN?
WELL, IT TOLD ME HOW TO GET OUT OF HERE, BUT I DON'T GET IT!
UH, LET'S SEE... "HE WHO ENTERED BY THE 'A' WILL EXIT BY THE 'A'"... IT'S NOT VERY CLEAR.
AND WHAT ARE THE "SHIPWRECK LAMPS"?
NO IDEA!
I HAVE TO SAY THAT I RARELY GO OUT AT NIGHT. IT'S DANGEROUS TO GO OUT AT NIGHT ON THIS ISLAND. AHHHHHH...
IT'S TIME TO GO TO BED! WE'LL SPEAK OF ALL THIS AGAIN TOMORROW.
YAWN...
FRIDAY WILL SHOW YOU TO YOUR ROOM.
IF THE GENTLEMAN WILL BE SO KIND AS TO FOLLOW ME...
UM... ARE THERE A LOT OF ROOMS?
EIGHT HUNDRED NINETY-TWO! I SHOULD KNOW—I DO ALL THE HOUSEWORK!
500
SO MAKE SURE TO PUT SLIPPERS ON YOUR FEET, BECAUSE I'VE HAD IT WITH WAXING THE FLOORS!
712
FRED

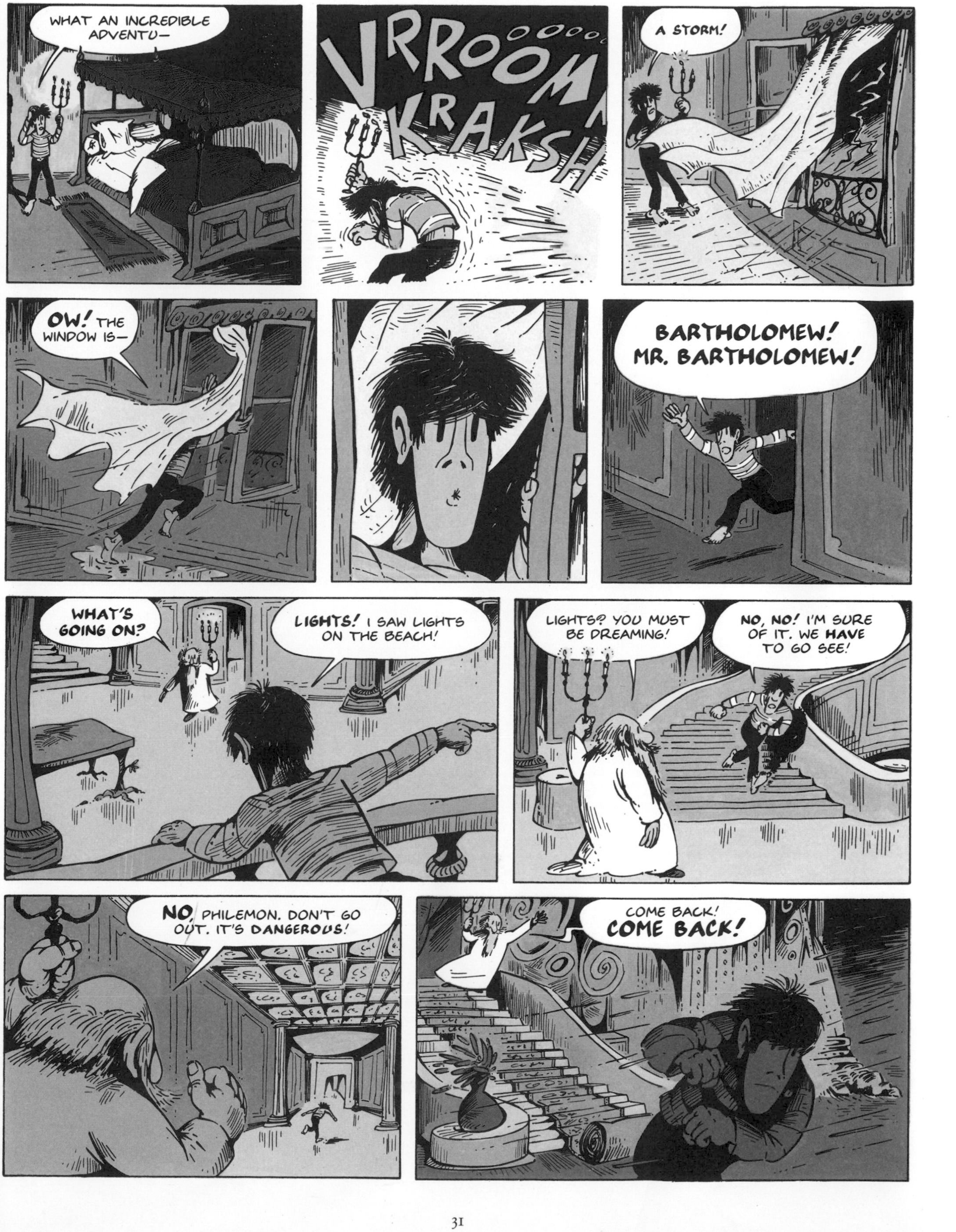
WHAT AN INCREDIBLE ADVENTU—
VRROOOOOOM
KRAKSH
A STORM!
OW! THE WINDOW IS—
BARTHOLOMEW! MR. BARTHOLOMEW!
WHAT'S GOING ON?
LIGHTS! I SAW LIGHTS ON THE BEACH!
LIGHTS? YOU MUST BE DREAMING!
NO, NO! I'M SURE OF IT. WE HAVE TO GO SEE!
NO, PHILEMON. DON'T GO OUT. IT'S DANGEROUS!
COME BACK! COME BACK!

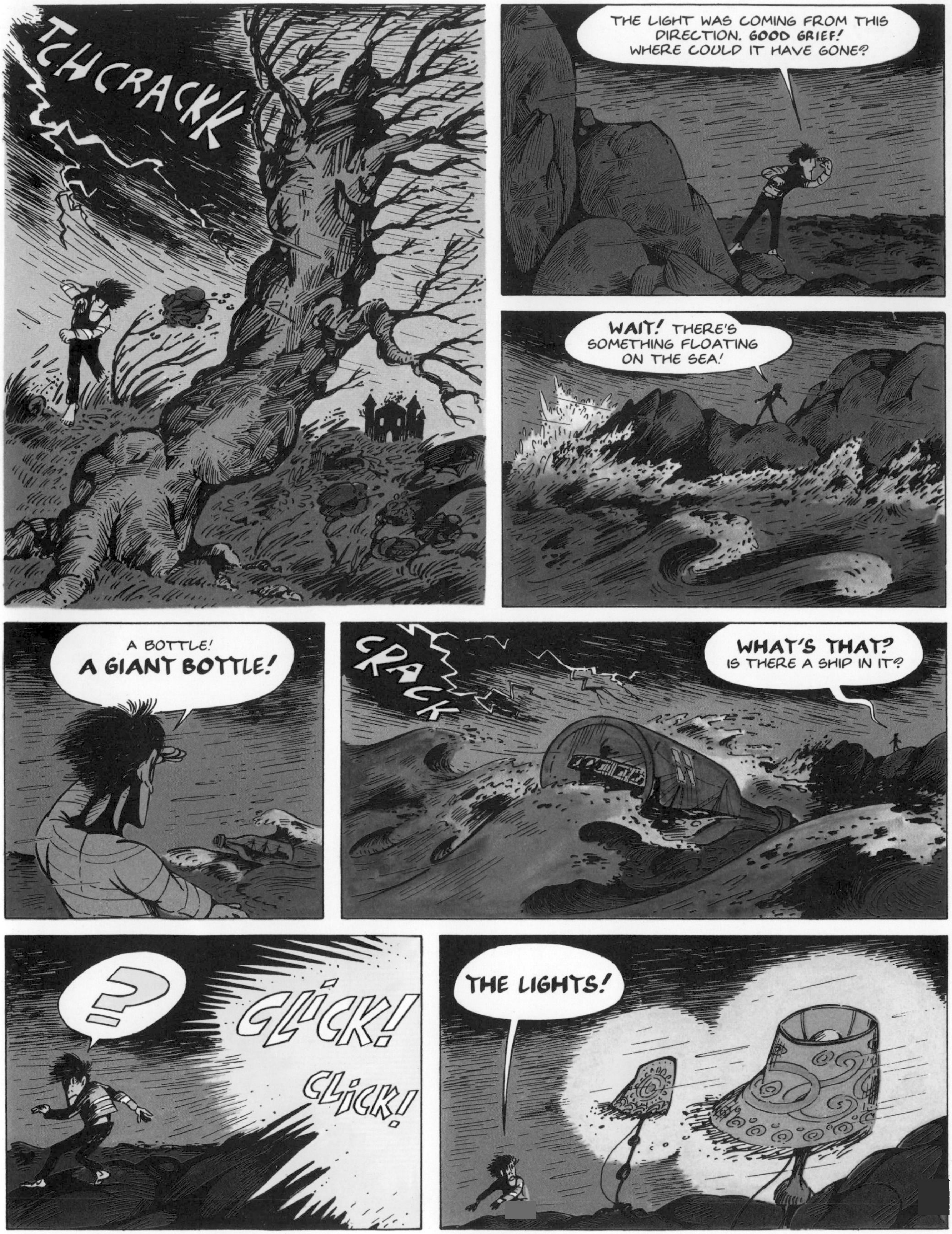
TCHCRACKK
THE LIGHT WAS COMING FROM THIS DIRECTION. GOOD GRIEF! WHERE COULD IT HAVE GONE?
WAIT! THERE'S SOMETHING FLOATING ON THE SEA!
A BOTTLE! A GIANT BOTTLE!
CRACK
WHAT'S THAT? IS THERE A SHIP IN IT?
?
CLICK!
CLICK!
THE LIGHTS!

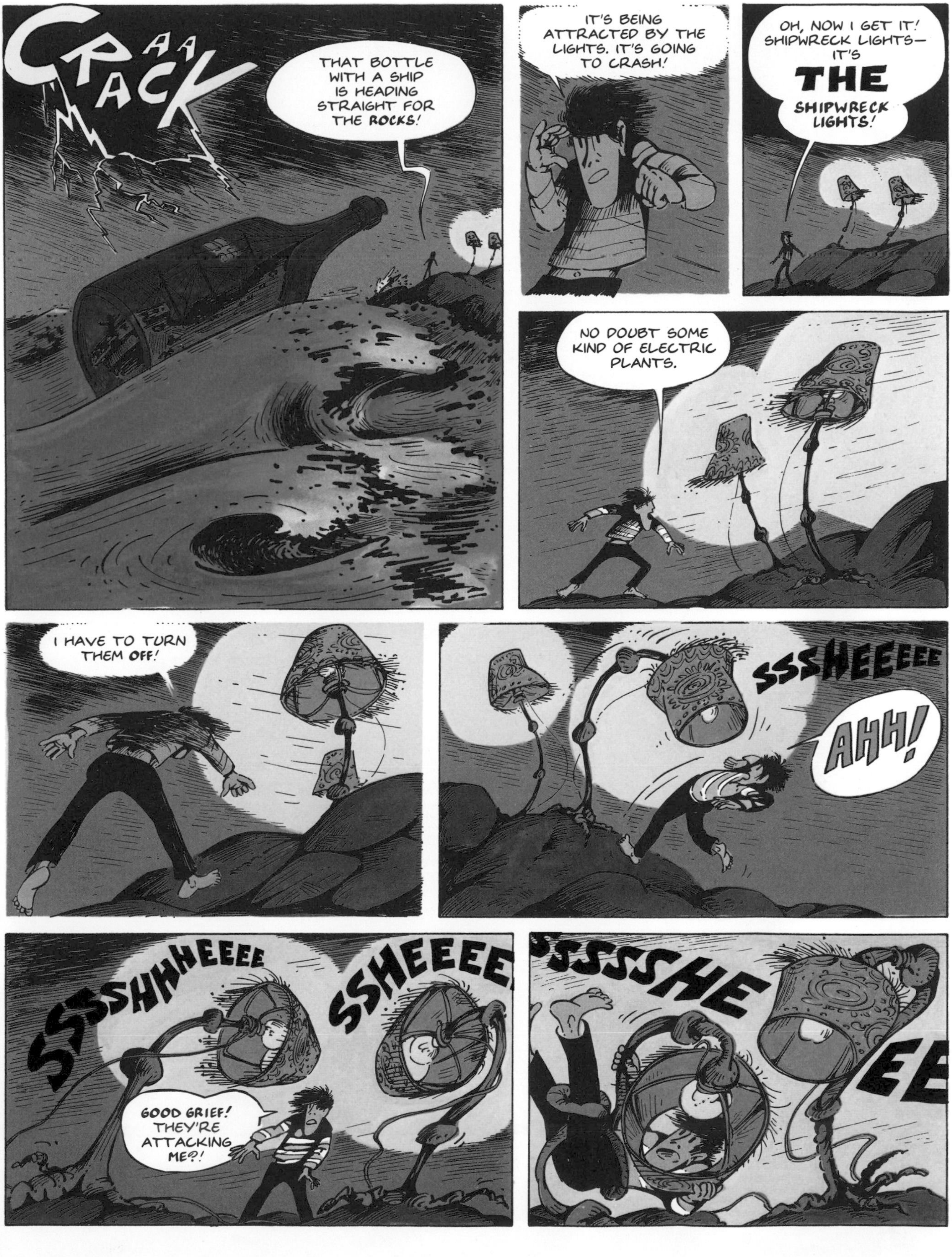
CRAAACK
THAT BOTTLE WITH A SHIP IS HEADING STRAIGHT FOR THE ROCKS!
IT'S BEING ATTRACTED BY THE LIGHTS. IT'S GOING TO CRASH!
OH, NOW I GET IT! SHIPWRECK LIGHTS— IT'S THE SHIPWRECK LIGHTS!
NO DOUBT SOME KIND OF ELECTRIC PLANTS.
I HAVE TO TURN THEM OFF!
SSSHEEEEEE
AHH!
SSSSHHHEEEEE
SSHEEEEE
GOOD GRIEF! THEY'RE ATTACKING ME?!
SSSSSHE
EE

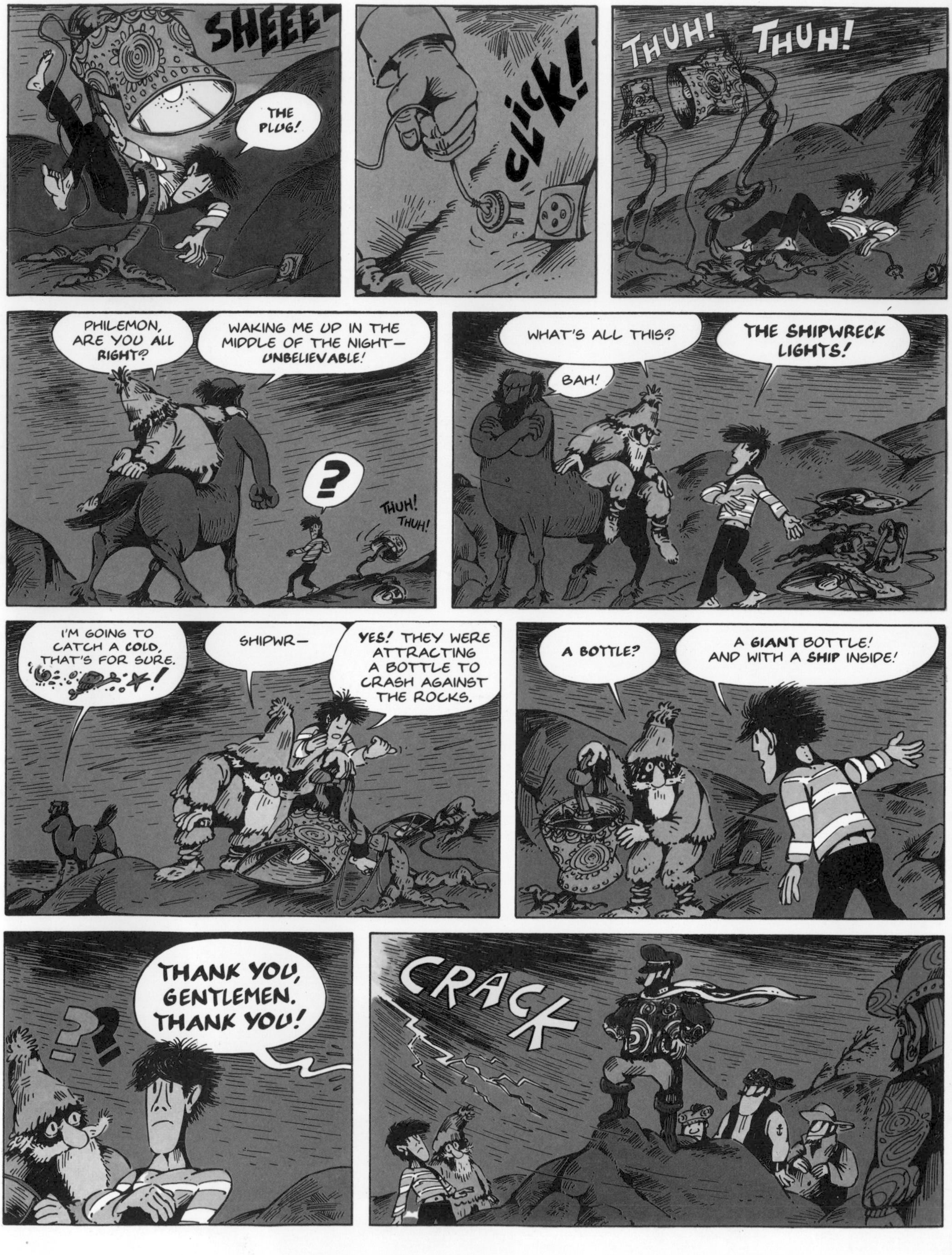

SHEEE
THE PLUG!
CLICK!
THUH! THUH!
PHILEMON, ARE YOU ALL RIGHT?
WAKING ME UP IN THE MIDDLE OF THE NIGHT— UNBELIEVABLE!
?
THUH! THUH!
WHAT'S ALL THIS?
BAH!
THE SHIPWRECK LIGHTS!
I'M GOING TO CATCH A COLD, THAT'S FOR SURE.
SHIPWR—
YES! THEY WERE ATTRACTING A BOTTLE TO CRASH AGAINST THE ROCKS.
A BOTTLE?
A GIANT BOTTLE! AND WITH A SHIP INSIDE!
??
THANK YOU, GENTLEMEN. THANK YOU!
CRACK

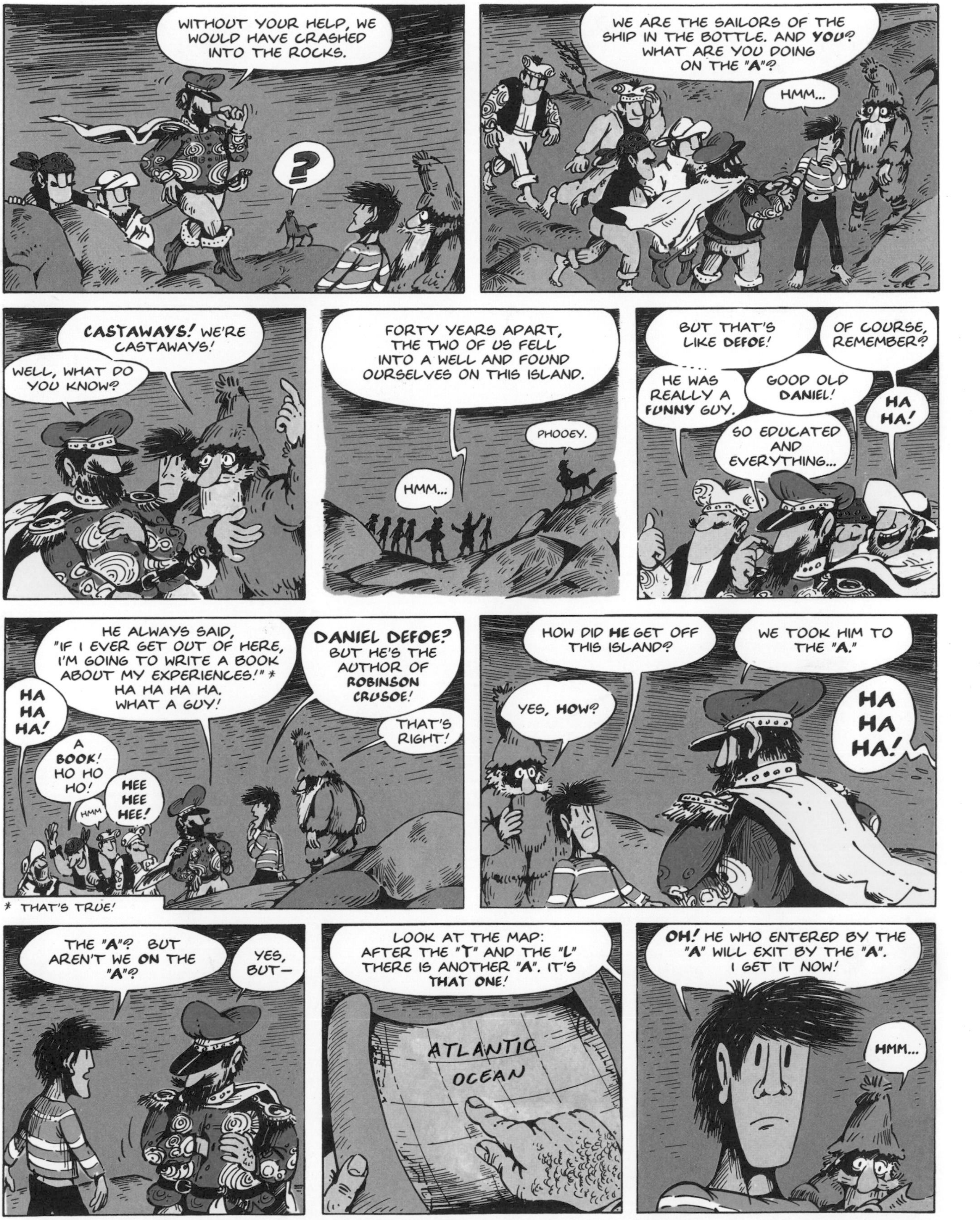

WITHOUT YOUR HELP, WE WOULD HAVE CRASHED INTO THE ROCKS.
?
WE ARE THE SAILORS OF THE SHIP IN THE BOTTLE. AND YOU? WHAT ARE YOU DOING ON THE "A"?
HMM...
CASTAWAYS! WE'RE CASTAWAYS!
WELL, WHAT DO YOU KNOW?
FORTY YEARS APART, THE TWO OF US FELL INTO A WELL AND FOUND OURSELVES ON THIS ISLAND.
PHOOEY.
HMM...
BUT THAT'S LIKE DEFOE!
OF COURSE, REMEMBER?
HE WAS REALLY A FUNNY GUY.
GOOD OLD DANIEL!
HA HA!
SO EDUCATED AND EVERYTHING...
HE ALWAYS SAID, "IF I EVER GET OUT OF HERE, I'M GOING TO WRITE A BOOK ABOUT MY EXPERIENCES!" * HA HA HA HA. WHAT A GUY!
HA HA HA!
DANIEL DEFOE? BUT HE'S THE AUTHOR OF ROBINSON CRUSOE!
THAT'S RIGHT!
A BOOK! HO HO HO!
HMM
HEE HEE HEE!
* THAT'S TRUE!
HOW DID HE GET OFF THIS ISLAND?
WE TOOK HIM TO THE "A."
YES, HOW?
HA HA HA!
THE "A"? BUT AREN'T WE ON THE "A"?
YES, BUT—
LOOK AT THE MAP: AFTER THE "T" AND THE "L" THERE IS ANOTHER "A". IT'S THAT ONE!
ATLANTIC OCEAN
OH! HE WHO ENTERED BY THE "A" WILL EXIT BY THE "A". I GET IT NOW!
HMM...

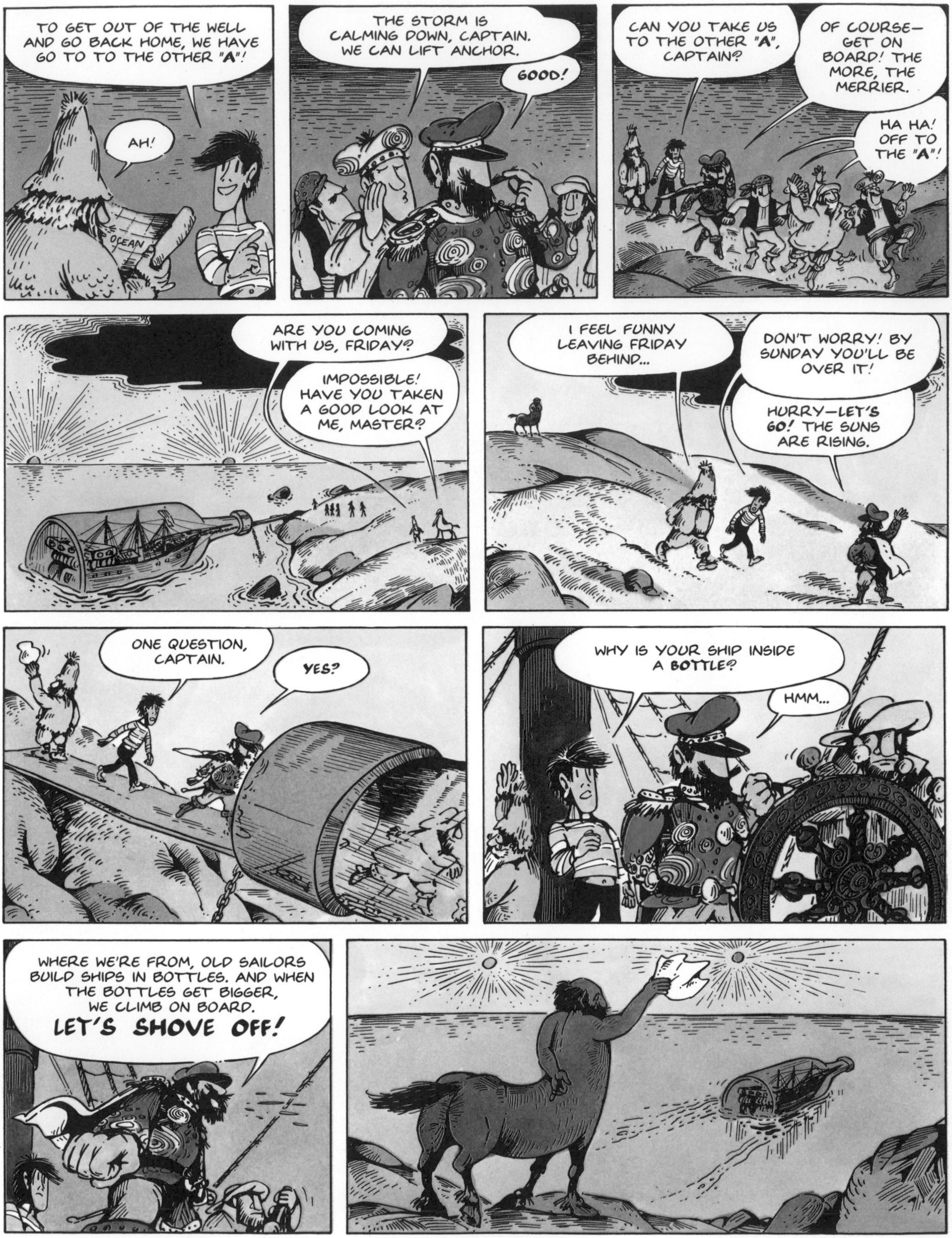
TO GET OUT OF THE WELL AND GO BACK HOME, WE HAVE GO TO TO THE OTHER "A"!
AH!
OCEAN
THE STORM IS CALMING DOWN, CAPTAIN. WE CAN LIFT ANCHOR.
GOOD!
CAN YOU TAKE US TO THE OTHER "A", CAPTAIN?
OF COURSE— GET ON BOARD! THE MORE, THE MERRIER.
HA HA! OFF TO THE "A"!
ARE YOU COMING WITH US, FRIDAY?
IMPOSSIBLE! HAVE YOU TAKEN A GOOD LOOK AT ME, MASTER?
I FEEL FUNNY LEAVING FRIDAY BEHIND...
DON'T WORRY! BY SUNDAY YOU'LL BE OVER IT!
HURRY—LET'S GO! THE SUNS ARE RISING.
ONE QUESTION, CAPTAIN.
YES?
WHY IS YOUR SHIP INSIDE A BOTTLE?
HMM...
WHERE WE'RE FROM, OLD SAILORS BUILD SHIPS IN BOTTLES. AND WHEN THE BOTTLES GET BIGGER, WE CLIMB ON BOARD.
LET'S SHOVE OFF!

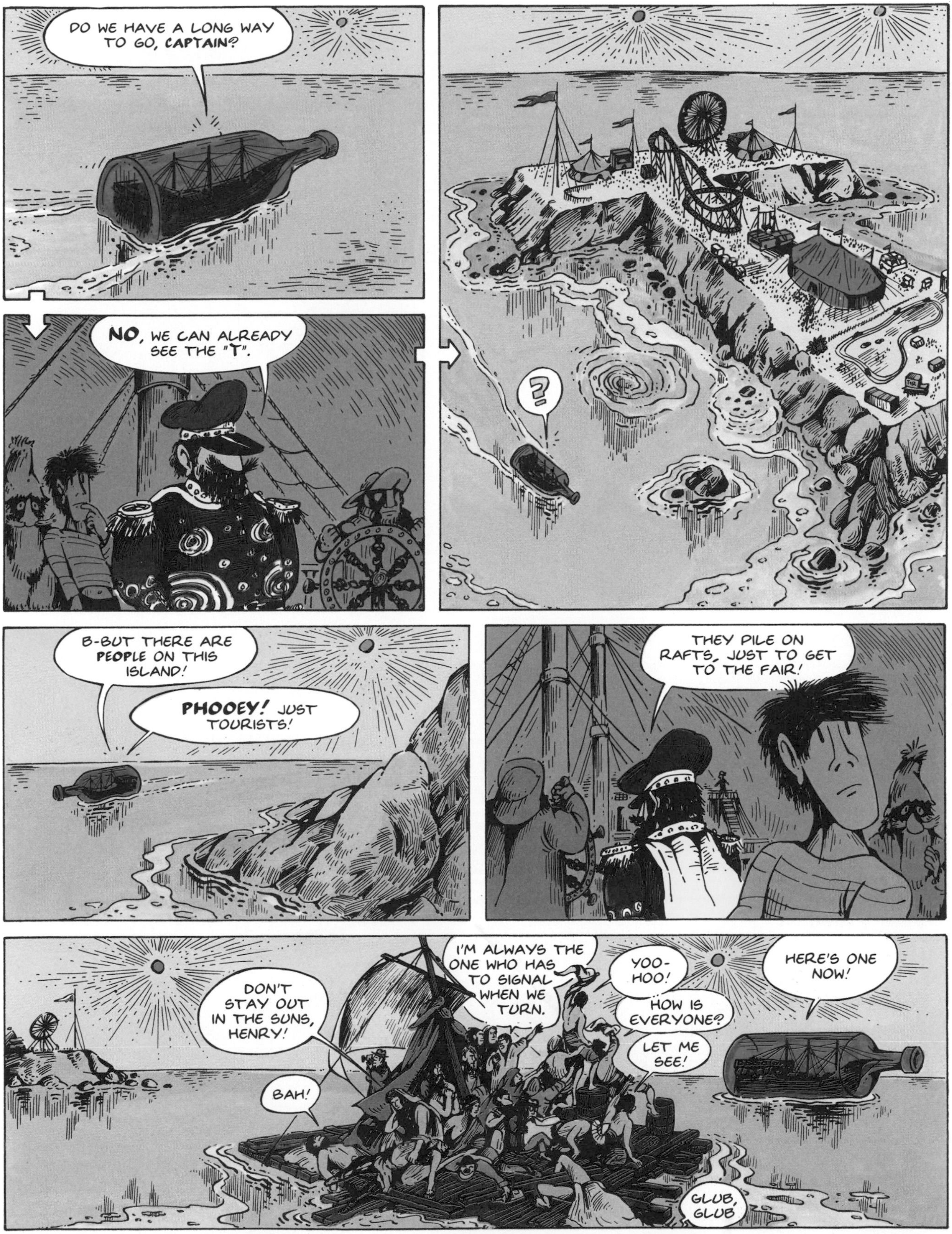
DO WE HAVE A LONG WAY TO GO, CAPTAIN?
NO, WE CAN ALREADY SEE THE "T".
?
B-BUT THERE ARE PEOPLE ON THIS ISLAND!
PHOOEY! JUST TOURISTS!
THEY PILE ON RAFTS, JUST TO GET TO THE FAIR!
DON'T STAY OUT IN THE SUNS, HENRY!
BAH!
I'M ALWAYS THE ONE WHO HAS TO SIGNAL WHEN WE TURN.
YOO-HOO!
HOW IS EVERYONE?
LET ME SEE!
GLUB, GLUB
HERE'S ONE NOW!

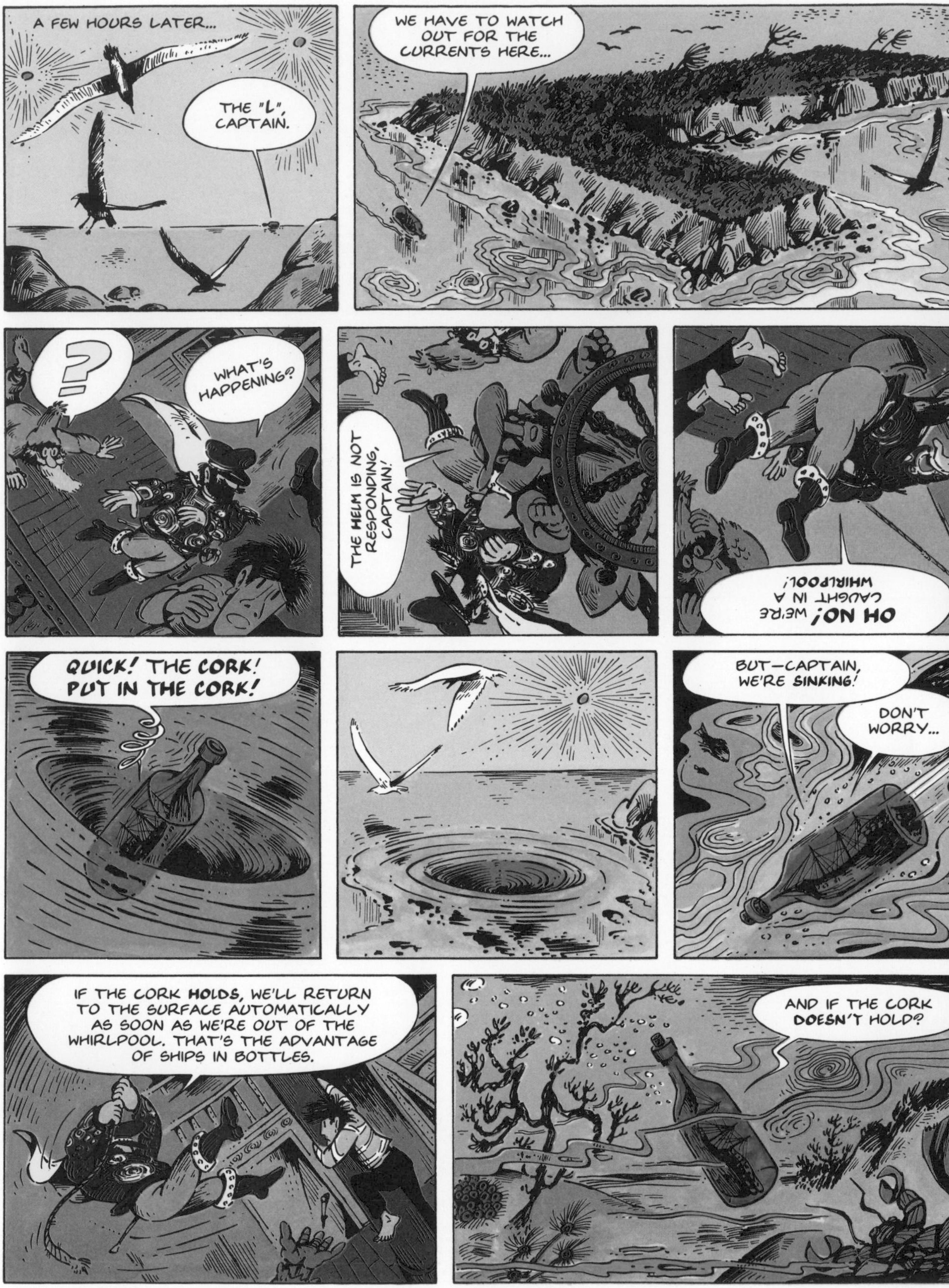
A FEW HOURS LATER...
THE "L", CAPTAIN.
WE HAVE TO WATCH OUT FOR THE CURRENTS HERE...
?
WHAT'S HAPPENING?
THE HELM IS NOT RESPONDING, CAPTAIN!
OH NO! WE'RE CAUGHT IN A WHIRLPOOL!
QUICK! THE CORK! PUT IN THE CORK!
BUT—CAPTAIN, WE'RE SINKING!
DON'T WORRY...
IF THE CORK HOLDS, WE'LL RETURN TO THE SURFACE AUTOMATICALLY AS SOON AS WE'RE OUT OF THE WHIRLPOOL. THAT'S THE ADVANTAGE OF SHIPS IN BOTTLES.
AND IF THE CORK DOESN'T HOLD?

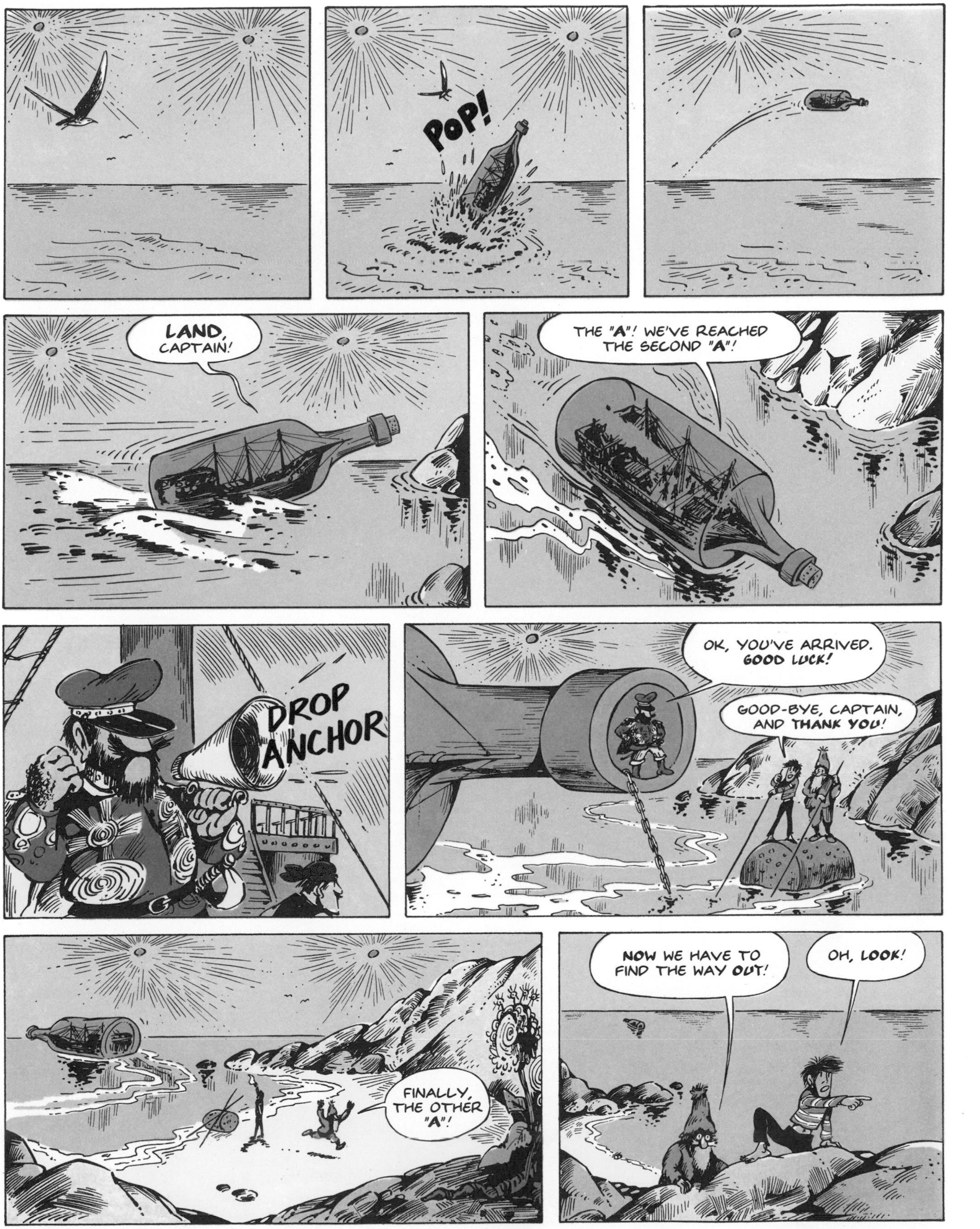
POP!
LAND, CAPTAIN!
THE "A"! WE'VE REACHED THE SECOND "A"!
DROP ANCHOR
OK, YOU'VE ARRIVED. GOOD LUCK!
GOOD-BYE, CAPTAIN, AND THANK YOU!
FINALLY, THE OTHER "A"!
NOW WE HAVE TO FIND THE WAY OUT!
OH, LOOK!

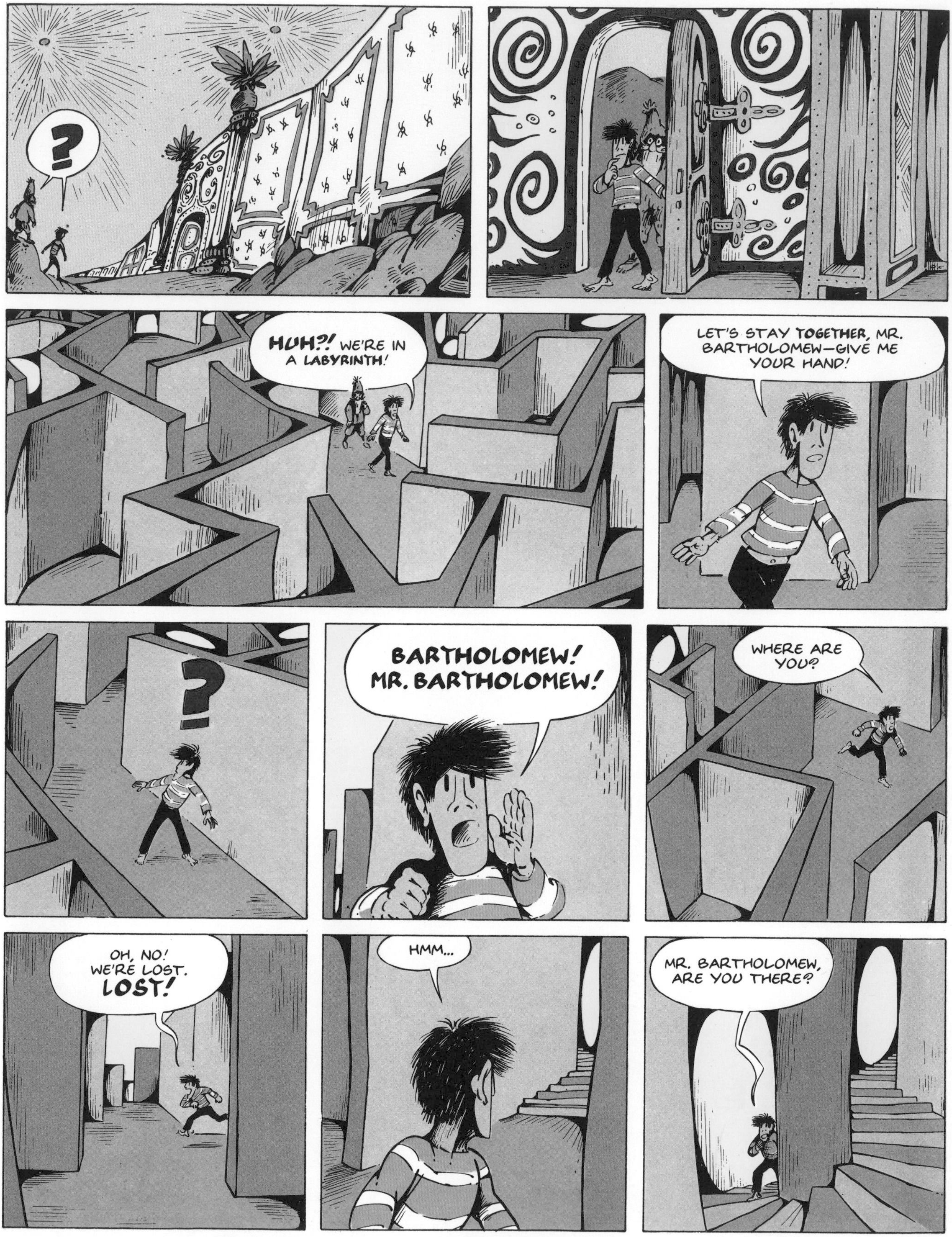
?
HUH?! WE'RE IN A LABYRINTH!
LET'S STAY TOGETHER, MR. BARTHOLOMEW—GIVE ME YOUR HAND!
?
BARTHOLOMEW! MR. BARTHOLOMEW!
WHERE ARE YOU?
OH, NO! WE'RE LOST. LOST!
HMM...
MR. BARTHOLOMEW, ARE YOU THERE?

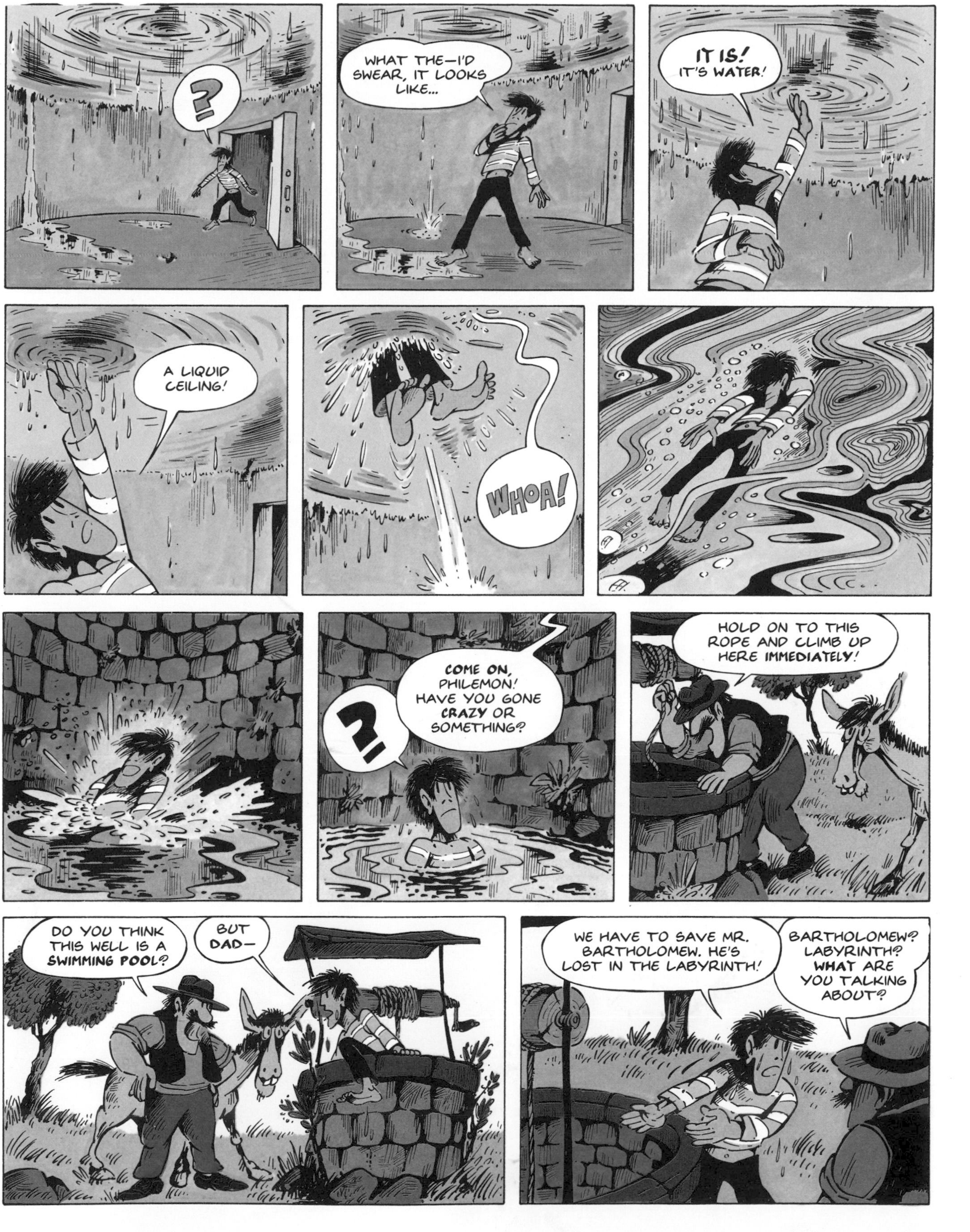
?
WHAT THE—I'D SWEAR, IT LOOKS LIKE...
IT IS! IT'S WATER!
A LIQUID CEILING!
WHOA!
COME ON, PHILEMON! HAVE YOU GONE CRAZY OR SOMETHING?
?
HOLD ON TO THIS ROPE AND CLIMB UP HERE IMMEDIATELY!
DO YOU THINK THIS WELL IS A SWIMMING POOL?
BUT DAD—
WE HAVE TO SAVE MR. BARTHOLOMEW. HE'S LOST IN THE LABYRINTH!
BARTHOLOMEW? LABYRINTH? WHAT ARE YOU TALKING ABOUT?

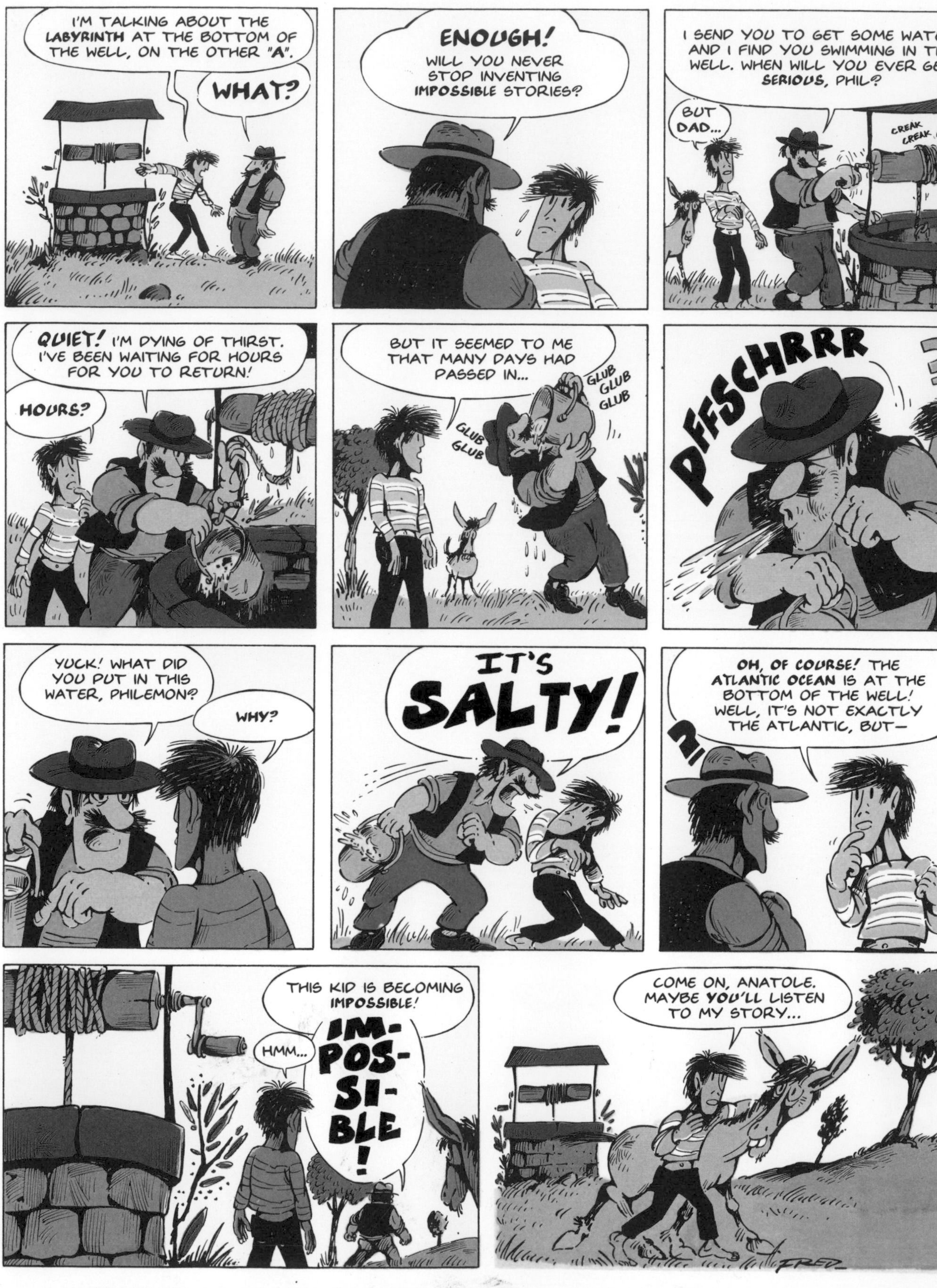

I'M TALKING ABOUT THE LABYRINTH AT THE BOTTOM OF THE WELL, ON THE OTHER "A".
WHAT?
ENOUGH! WILL YOU NEVER STOP INVENTING IMPOSSIBLE STORIES?
I SEND YOU TO GET SOME WATER, AND I FIND YOU SWIMMING IN THE WELL. WHEN WILL YOU EVER GET SERIOUS, PHIL?
BUT DAD...
CREAK CREAK CREAK
QUIET! I'M DYING OF THIRST. I'VE BEEN WAITING FOR HOURS FOR YOU TO RETURN!
HOURS?
BUT IT SEEMED TO ME THAT MANY DAYS HAD PASSED IN...
GLUB GLUB GLUB
GLUB GLUB
PFFSCHRRR
?
YUCK! WHAT DID YOU PUT IN THIS WATER, PHILEMON?
WHY?
IT'S SALTY!
OH, OF COURSE! THE ATLANTIC OCEAN IS AT THE BOTTOM OF THE WELL! WELL, IT'S NOT EXACTLY THE ATLANTIC, BUT—
?
THIS KID IS BECOMING IMPOSSIBLE!
HMM...
IM-POS-SI-BLE!
COME ON, ANATOLE. MAYBE YOU'LL LISTEN TO MY STORY...
FRED

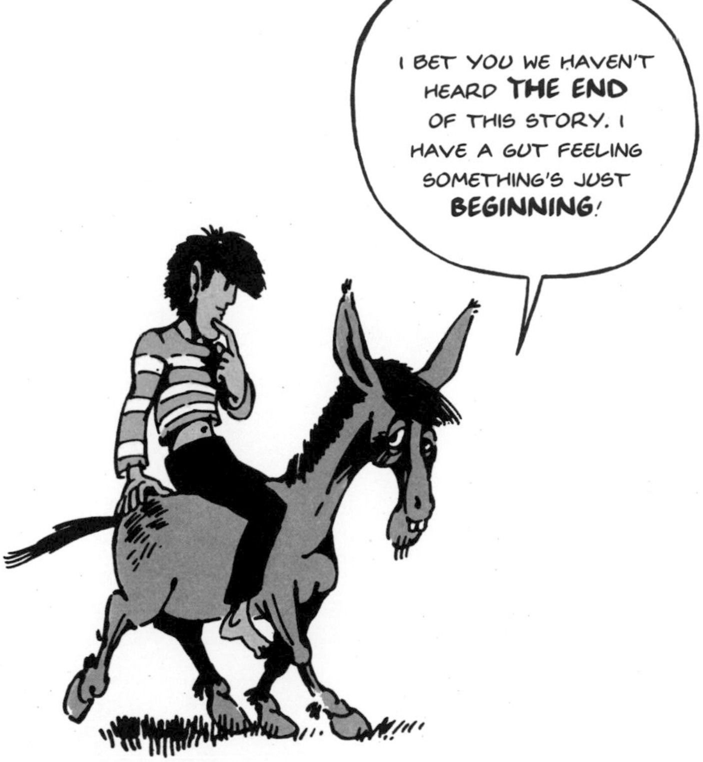
I BET YOU WE HAVEN'T HEARD **THE END** OF THIS STORY. I HAVE A GUT FEELING SOMETHING'S JUST **BEGINNING**!

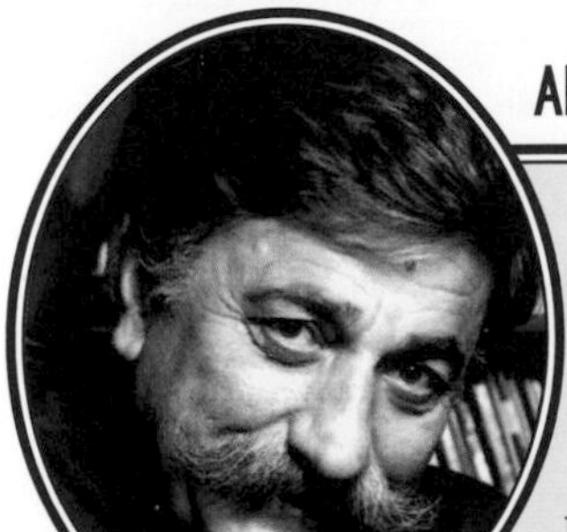

ABOUT THE AUTHOR

Frédéric Othon Aristidès (1931-2013), known as Fred, is one of France's most influential and revered cartoonists. When he was young, he loved to read Edgar Allan Poe, Charles Dickens, and Oscar Wilde. In the sixties, Fred co-founded *Hara-Kiri*, the leading satirical publication of the May '68 movement–he designed its first 60 covers. Philémon, his story for young readers, was first published in *Pilote* in 1972 by René Goscinny, the author of the Astérix series. Philémon is Fred's most celebrated creation: millions of young French people have grown up with it, and it has inspired many of today's most talented cartoonists. The sixteenth and final volume of Philémon was released in 2013, before Fred's passing. Fred also got to see the beginnings of a Philémon movie, which is currently in the works. While there's no knowing where he found his inspiration, he said he often got his best ideas while taking a bath.

Down the well, in a world of utter fantasy...

As a teenager growing up in Paris in the late sixties, I remember few pleasures–life was mostly a grind of memorization and dull schoolwork. But one day of the week stood out: every Tuesday I'd go out with my dad to the corner newsstand to get a comics magazine, *Pilote*. At the time, I devoured books–I would read as I walked to school and wouldn't even stop to cross the street–but for *Pilote* I slowed down. I took it home and would only look at it while lying down, the door locked. I'd slog through the dull adventure strips first, getting them out of the way so I could get to my favorite humor strips like Astérix or Lucky Luke, and last of all, Fred's adventures of Philémon. I knew that in that first slow, careful reading, and every re-reading after that, I would be rewarded with a wealth of hidden treasures. Fred was a formalist and a deconstructionist, an author who beckoned me, the reader, to enter into the game with him. He lifted the panel borders just enough so you could see the tail of his magician's coat disappear every time you peeked. He opened up a world which has not ceased to delight me ever since. But as quirky and individual as Fred's world is, it is rooted in a deep well of fantasy, a few elements of which we tried to note here.

Pilote
LE NAUFRAGÉ DU A

–Françoise Mouly, Art Editor, *The New Yorker*

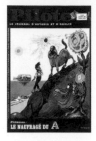

PHILEMON – The name comes from the ancient Greek Φιλήμων, which means only or "best friend". According to the Roman poet Ovid, Philemon and his wife Baucis were a poor, old, and loving couple who lived in Asia Minor and welcomed two strangers into their home when no one else in their town would. The two men turned out to be Zeus and his son Hermes. Zeus led Philemon and Baucis up a hill, where they watched as the god destroyed the town to punish the people for their lack of hospitality (which was considered very important in ancient times). Zeus rewarded Philemon and Baucis for their generosity by making them the guardians of a temple he created where their home stood. When offered a wish, the couple asked Zeus if, when their time came, they could die at the same moment. Zeus granted it: during their last breaths, they were transformed into intertwined trees.

OH! A TASTY-LOOKING THISTLE!
SLURP!

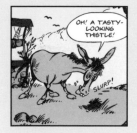

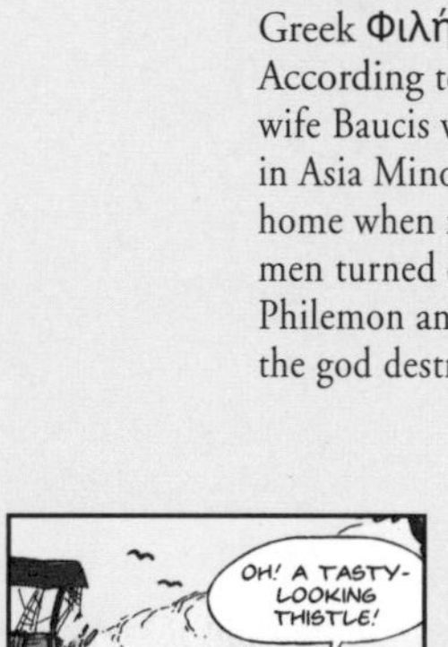

ANATOLE *(page 12)* – Anatole is not the only wise talking donkey. In the Bible, Balaam rides a donkey who goes off the road after it sees an angel barring their path. Balaam beats the donkey before the animal starts talking to him. The donkey explains he has saved his master's life–the angel was there to kill Balaam for his wickedness.

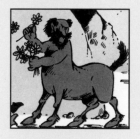

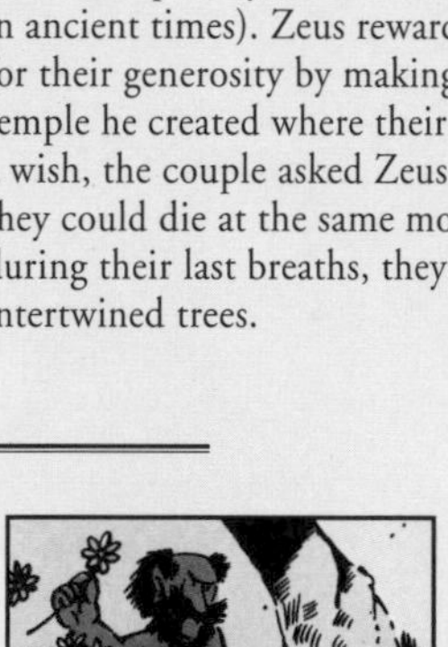

FRIDAY *(page 20)* – Friday is the name of a servant in Daniel Defoe's book *Robinson Crusoe*. In the Philemon story, Friday is a centaur, a creature from Greek mythology with the head and torso of a human and the legs of a horse. Centaurs appear in The Chronicles of Narnia, the Harry Potter series, and in Percy Jackson and the Olympians.

NOTHING. I SEE NOTHING!

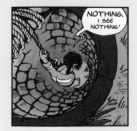

WISHING WELLS *(page 13)* – In Norse mythology, there was a Well of Wisdom, known as Mimir's Well, which would make you wise if you sacrificed something to it. The god Odin threw in his right eye to receive great wisdom. In German and Celtic folklore, wells were believed to grant wishes because gods lived at the bottom of them.

CRACK!

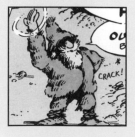

MR. BARTHOLOMEW *(page 21)*– Bartholomew is probably dressed in green because he made his clothes from plants, just like Robinson Crusoe. Leprechauns, a kind of fairy from Irish folklore, also dress in green. They usually look like old men and spend most of their time making shoes. They hide their gold coins in pots at the end of rainbows. If you catch one, he will grant you three wishes in exchange for his freedom.

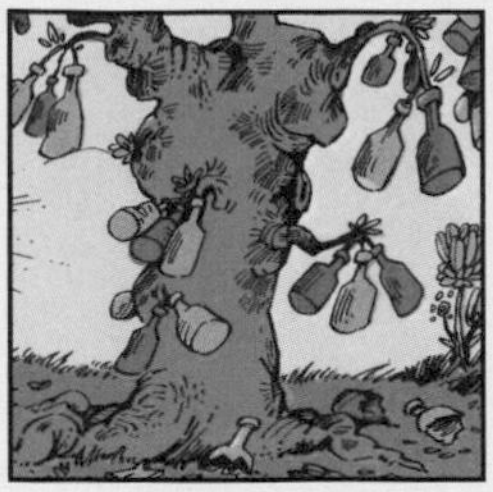

STRANGE PLANTS *(page 23)* – You'll see a lot of strange plants growing in the pages of this book. You can also find strange plants in the works of Edward Lear, Lewis Carroll, Dr. Seuss, and in *Little Shop of Horrors*. There are also plenty of strange plants in the natural world: the pitcher plant, the Venus flytrap, and the different species of *Rafflesia*, to name a few.

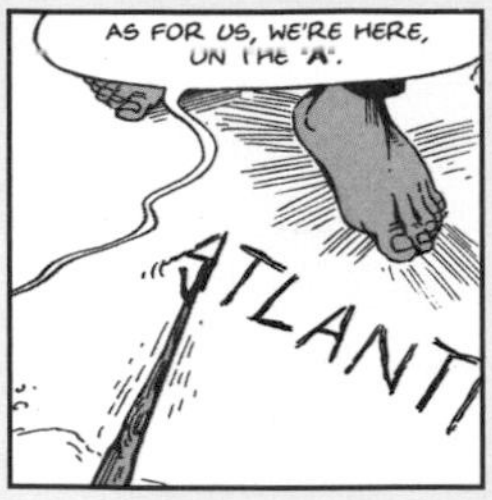
AS FOR US, WE'RE HERE, ON THE "A".
ATLANTI

ATLANTIC OCEAN *(page 24)* – The Atlantic Ocean lies between the west coast of North and South America and the east coast of Europe and Africa. The Ancient Greeks believed it was a great river that encircled the world. They called it *Atlantis Thalassa*, which means the "Sea of Atlas." They also called its southern part the "Ethiopic" Ocean, even though it is nowhere near Ethiopia.

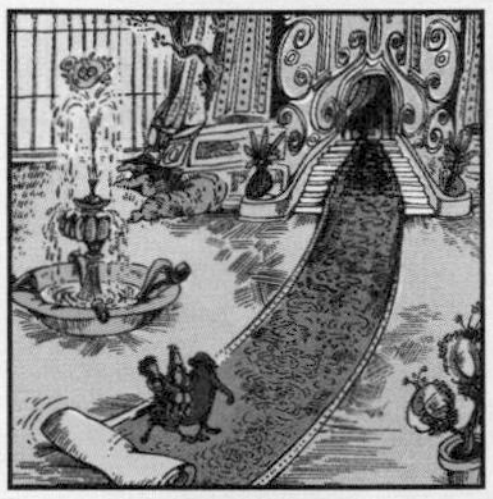

RED CARPET *(page 25)* – Red carpets are rolled out for royalty and VIPs (Very Important Persons), such as actors and directors going to the Oscars. In an Ancient Greek play, Agamemnon's angry wife Clytemnestra lays out a red carpet for him when he returns from the Trojan War. Agamemnon knows something is up, because red carpets are reserved for the gods.

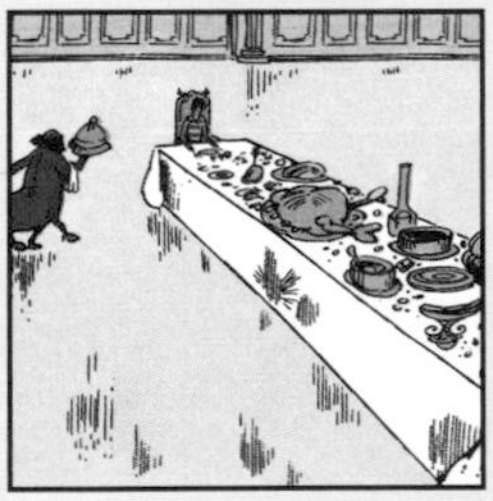

BANQUET TABLE *(page 28)* – Banquet tables are at the center of feast halls in Norse mythology. Your rank is indicated by how close you sit to the head of the table–and to the fire. In the Middle Ages, European kings and queens adorned banquet tables with a huge variety of delicious foods in all colors and flavors, served on plates of gold or silver.

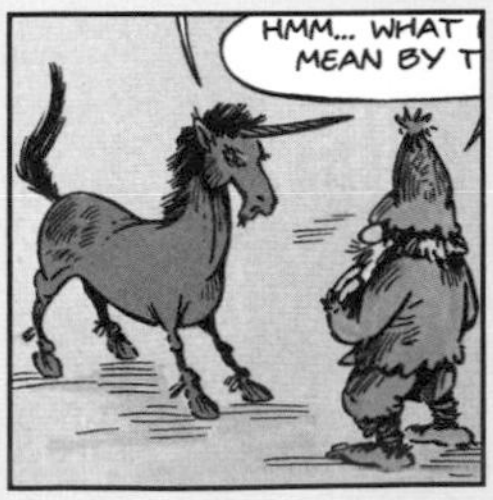
HMM... WHAT
MEAN BY T

UNICORNS *(page 29)* – In ancient times, the unicorn was thought to be a beast with a large, pointed, spiral horn on its head. In European folklore, unicorns were depicted as white horses with such horns. They lived in the woods and were symbols of purity. Belief held that their horn could make unclean water drinkable and heal sickness. You can see a beautiful series of unicorn tapestries at the Cloisters in New York City.

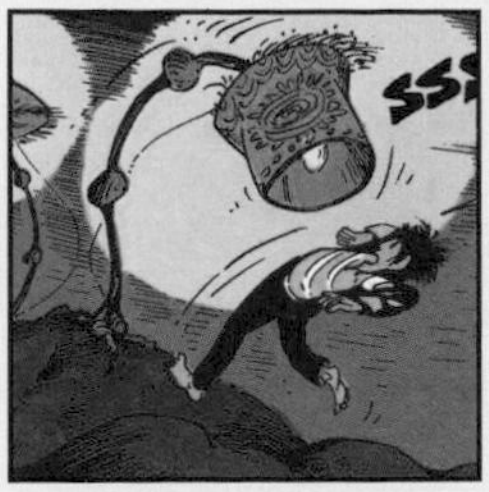

THE SHIPWRECK LIGHTS *(page 32)* – Fred might have gotten his idea for the shipwreck lamps from the will-o'-the-wisp, mysterious lights seen by travelers at night over marshes and swamps. These lights flicker and draw people away from safe paths. They appear mostly in English and European folklore.

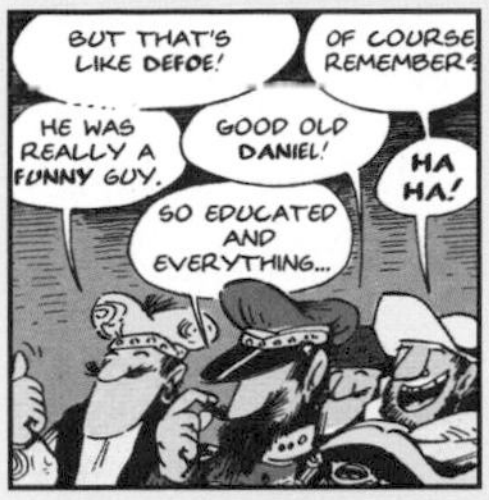
BUT THAT'S LIKE DEFOE!
OF COURSE REMEMBER
HE WAS REALLY A FUNNY GUY.
GOOD OLD DANIEL!
HA HA!
SO EDUCATED AND EVERYTHING...

DANIEL DEFOE *(page 35)* – Daniel Defoe, an Englishman, is the author of *Robinson Crusoe*, the story of a man shipwrecked on a desert island with his faithful servant, Friday. It is partially based on a true story. In the first 1719 edition, Crusoe is credited as the author, leading many readers of the time to believe that he was a real person.

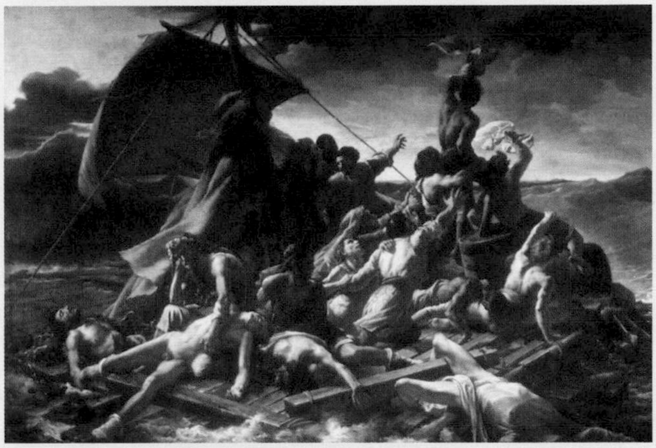

RAFT OF THE MEDUSA *(page 37)* – In 1816, the French boat *Méduse (Medusa)* ran aground off the coast of present-day Mauritania, in Africa. A raft was constructed and about 150 people crowded on. Only 15 survived the 13 days at sea. The French Romantic painter Théodore Géricault depicted this historical event in a huge, dramatic painting. In Greek mythology, Medusa was a monster with a woman's face and venomous snakes for hair. If you looked at her directly, you turned to stone.

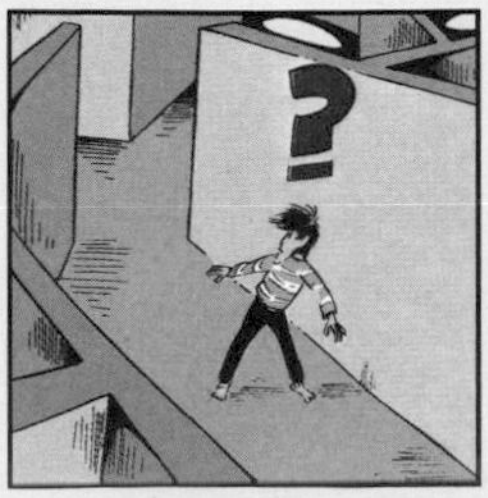

LABYRINTH *(page 40)* – Minos, King of ancient Crete, had a labyrinth, or maze, constructed by the architect Daedalus to hide the Minotaur, a creature half-bull and half-human. No one who entered the labyrinth ever came out–the Minotaur ate them all. Theseus finally put an end to this terrible curse when he killed the Minotaur. The word "labyrinth" can be used to describe any kind of complicated arrangement.

Tips for Parents, Teachers, and Librarians:
TOON GRAPHICS FOR VISUAL READERS

TOON Graphics are comics and visual narratives that bring the text to life in a way that captures young readers' imaginations and makes them want to read on—and read more. When the authors are also artists, they can convey their creative vision with pictures as well as words. They can enhance the overarching theme and present important details that are absorbed by the reader along with the text. Young readers also develop their aesthetic sense when they experience the relationship of text to picture in all its communicative power.

Reading TOON Graphics is a pleasure for all. Beginners and seasoned readers alike will sharpen both their literal and inferential reading skills.

Let the pictures tell the story

The very economy of comic books necessitates the use of a reader's imaginative powers. In comics, the images often imply rather than tell outright. Readers must learn to make connections between events to complete the narrative, helping them build their ability to visualize and to make "mental maps."

A comic book also gives readers a great deal of visual context that can be used to investigate the thinking behind the characters' choices.

Pay attention to the artist's choices

Look carefully at the artwork: it offers a subtext that at first is sensed only on a subliminal level by the reader and encourages rereading. It creates a sense of continuity for the action, and it can tell you about the art, architecture, and clothing of a specific time period. It may present the atmosphere, landscape, and flora and fauna of another time or of another part of the world. TOON Graphics can also present multiple points of view and simultaneous events in a manner not permitted by linear written narration. Facial expressions and body language reveal subtle aspects of characters' personalities beyond what can be expressed by words.

Read and reread!

Readers can compare comic book artists' styles and evaluate how different authors get their point across in different ways. In investigating the author's choices, a young reader begins to gain a sense of how all literary and art forms can be used to convey the author's central ideas.

The world of TOON Graphics and of comic book art is rich and varied. Making meaning out of reading with the aid of visuals may be the best way to become a lifelong reader, one who knows how to read for pleasure and for information—a reader who *loves* to read.

A few nibbles for thought...

• After Philemon asks, "What time is it?" *(page 19)*, a clock appears two panels later. What does this tell you about the place where Philemon has found himself? What expectations do you now have for this story?

• This story is full of comic misunderstandings, as when Philemon and Bartholomew talk about bottles falling from trees *(page 23)*. Identify some of these misunderstandings and explain how they drive the story.

• The unicorn delivers a prophecy *(page 29)*. Why do you think the author chose to include a prophecy in this story? Can you think of other stories involving prophecies, warnings, or coded instructions?